MIDWIVES ON-CALL

Welcome to Melbourne Victoria Hospital—
and to the exceptional midwives
who make up the Melbourne Maternity Unit!

These midwives in a million work miracles
on a daily basis, delivering tiny bundles of joy
into the arms of their brand-new mums!

Amidst the drama and emotion of babies
arriving at all hours of the day and night, when
the shifts are over, somehow there's still time
for some sizzling out-of-hours romance…

Whilst these caring professionals might come
face-to-face with a whole lot of love in their
line of work, now it's their turn to find
a happy-ever-after of their own!

Midwives On-Call

Midwives, mothers and babies—
lives changing for ever…!

Dear Reader,

Have you ever met someone and formed an instant opinion—only to be forced to revise that opinion once you get to know them? That's the case when obstetrician Darcie Green meets gorgeous Lucas Elliot for the first time. Sparks fly, and she soon labels him a playboy of the worst kind, only interested in one thing. Darcie has no intention of joining the throngs of female patients and co-workers who seem to hang on his every word. What she *doesn't* realise, however, is that Lucas uses his flirtatious charm to conceal a painful family secret and his real reason for becoming a midwife.

Thank you for joining Lucas and Darcie as they tiptoe around their attraction and try their best to avoid repeating the mistakes of the past. And maybe, *just maybe*, this very special couple will discover what love and loyalty really mean. I hope you enjoy reading their story as much as I loved writing it!

Love

Tina Beckett

HER PLAYBOY'S SECRET

BY
TINA BECKETT

First published in Great Britain 2015
by Mills & Boon, an imprint of Harlequin (UK) Limited,
Large Print edition 2016
Eton House, 18-24 Paradise Road,
Richmond, Surrey, TW9 1SR

© 2015 Harlequin Books S.A.

Special thanks and acknowledgement are given
to Tina Beckett for her contribution to the
Midwives On-Call series.

ISBN: 978-0-263-26069-4

Printed and bound in Great Britain
by CPI Antony Rowe, Chippenham, Wiltshire

To those who dare to chase their dreams

Born to a family that was always on the move, **Tina Beckett** learned to pack a suitcase almost before she knew how to tie her shoes. Fortunately she met a man who also loved to travel, and she snapped him right up. Married for over twenty years, Tina has three wonderful children and has lived in gorgeous places such as Portugal and Brazil.

Living where English reading material is difficult to find has its drawbacks, however. Tina had to come up with creative ways to satisfy her love for romance novels, so she picked up her pen and tried writing one. After her tenth book she realised she was hooked. She was officially a writer.

A three-times Golden Heart finalist, and fluent in Portuguese, Tina now divides her time between the United States and Brazil. She loves to use exotic locales as the backdrop for many of her stories. When she's not writing you can find her either on horseback or soldering stained-glass panels for her home.

Tina loves to hear from readers. You can contact her through her website or 'friend' her on Facebook.

Books by Tina Beckett

Mills & Boon Medical Romance

Hot Brazilian Docs!
To Play With Fire
The Dangers of Dating Dr Carvalho

One Night That Changed Everything
NYC Angels: Flirting with Danger
The Lone Wolf's Craving
Doctor's Guide to Dating in the Jungle
Her Hard to Resist Husband
His Girl From Nowhere
How to Find a Man in Five Dates
The Soldier She Could Never Forget

Visit the Author Profile page at millsandboon.co.uk for more titles.

MIDWIVES ON-CALL

Midwives, mothers and babies—
lives changing for ever...!

**Enter the magical world of the Melbourne Maternity Unit and
the exceptional midwives there, delivering tiny bundles of joy on a
daily basis. Now it's time to find a happy-ever-after of their own...**

Just One Night? by Carol Marinelli
Gorgeous Greek doctor Alessi Manos is determined
to charm the beautiful yet frosty Isla Delamere...
but can he melt this ice queen's heart?

Meant-To-Be Family by Marion Lennox
When Dr Oliver Evans's estranged wife, Emily, crashes back
into his life, old passions are reignited. But brilliant Dr Evans
is in for a surprise... Emily has two foster children!

Always the Midwife by Alison Roberts
Midwife Sophia Toulson and hard-working paramedic
Aiden Harrison share an explosive attraction...but will they
overcome their tragic pasts and take a chance on love?

Midwife's Baby Bump by Susanne Hampton
Hotshot surgeon Tristan Hamilton's passionate night
with pretty student midwife Flick has unexpected consequences!

Midwife...to Mum! by Sue MacKay
Free-spirited locum midwife Ally Parker
meets top GP and gorgeous single dad Flynn Reynolds.
Is she finally ready to settle down with a family of her own?

His Best Friend's Baby by Susan Carlisle
When beautiful redhead Phoebe Taylor turns up on ex-army medic
Ryan Matthews's doorstep there's only one thing keeping them apart:
she's his best friend's widow...and eight months pregnant!

Unlocking Her Surgeon's Heart by Fiona Lowe
Brooding city surgeon Noah Jackson
meets compassionate Outback midwife Lilia Cartwright.
Could Lilia be the key to Noah's locked-away heart?

Her Playboy's Secret by Tina Beckett
Renowned English obstetrician Darcie Green
might think playboy Lucas Elliot is nothing but trouble—
but is there more to this gorgeous doc than meets the eye?

Experience heartwarming emotion and pulse-racing drama in
Midwives On-Call
**this sensational eight-book continuity
from Mills & Boon Medical Romance**

**These books are also available in eBook format
from millsandboon.co.uk**

PROLOGUE

One week ago

IT WAS A curse heard around the world. Or at least around the ward of the Melbourne Maternity Unit.

Everyone on the ward went silent and several heads cranked around to see what the normally easygoing Lucas Elliot could possibly be upset about.

Darcie Green already knew—had braced herself for this very moment, wondering what his reaction would be.

Now she knew.

Still facing the rotation roster hanging on the far wall, Lucas didn't move for several seconds. Then, as if he couldn't quite believe what his eyes were telling him, one finger went to the chart, dragging across it to follow the line that matched dates with names.

She cringed as he muttered yet again, slightly lower this time. A few sympathetic glances came her way as people went back to their jobs. Isla Delamere, her former flatmate—now heavily pregnant—mouthed, "Sorry," as she tiptoed out of firing range.

A perfect beginning to a stellar day. She rolled her eyes.

Nine months in Australia and Darcie was just beginning to feel a part of the team. Except for Lucas's very vocal reaction at having the rota that matched hers, that was. He'd evidently not seen the list until just now.

Did he even know she was standing not seven meters behind him at the nurses' station? Probably not.

Then again, it was doubtful he would even care.

It wasn't as if she felt any better about having to spend an entire rotation with the handsome senior midwife. She just hadn't been quite as "loud" in expressing her displeasure.

Yes, she'd given him an earful about his periods of tardiness a few months back. But that had been no reason to call her an uptight, snooty, English…

Her eyes closed before the word formed, a flash of hurt working through her yet again.

Was the thought of being paired with her so hideous that he had to make sure everyone on the ward knew what he thought of her?

Evidently.

And why not? Her fiancé hadn't minded letting a whole chapel full of wedding guests know that he'd fallen in love with her best friend, who just so happened to be her maid of honor. Tabitha had promptly run over to him, squealing with delight, and thrown herself into his arms, leaving Darcie standing there in shock.

And, yes, Robert had called her uptight as well, right before he'd dropped the bomb that had ended their engagement.

Lucas's left hand went to the back of his neck, head bending forward as he massaged his muscles for a moment. When he finally turned around his eyes swept the area, going right past her before retracing his steps and pausing.

On her.

Then his left brow quirked, a rueful smile curving his lips. "Sorry. Heard that, did you?"

Was he serious? "I imagine there were very few who didn't."

He moved forward, until he was standing in front of her—all six feet of him. "I bet you did some name-calling of your own when you saw the rotation." His smile faded. "Unless you requested we work this one together."

Sure. That's just what she would have done, left to her own devices.

She forced her chin up. "No, I didn't request it, but it doesn't bother me, if that's what you mean. I've had worse assignments." Before she could congratulate herself on keeping her response cool and measured, even when her insides were squirming with embarrassment, he gave her a quick grin.

"Touché, Dr. Green. Although since you almost had me fired the last time we interacted, I assume your 'worse assignment' didn't fare quite as well."

Since the assignment she'd been referring to had had to do with returning hundreds of wedding gifts courtesy of her ex, it would appear that way. "I don't know about that. I think he feels *quite* lucky not to have to deal with my—how did you put it?—'uptight English ways' any more."

Lucas's gaze trailed over her face, but instead of whipping off a sharp retort he leaned in closer. "Then maybe you should consider some behavior modification courses."

Although the words were made in jest—at least she thought they were—they still stung. Darcie pulled the edges of her cardigan around herself to combat the chill spreading from her heart to the rest of her body and then forced every muscle in her chin go utterly still, so he wouldn't see the wobble. "You're right. Maybe I should."

His head tilted, and he studied her for a minute longer. He reached out a hand as if to touch her, before lowering it again. "Hey. Sorry. I was teasing."

Maybe, but a part of what he'd said was true. Men did seem to find her "chilly and distant"—words her ex had also used to describe her during the last troubled weeks of their engagement. And he had been right. Compared to her, Tabitha was warm and bubbly and anything but distant.

Darcie couldn't help the way she was made, though, could she? She dragged her thoughts back to the man in front of her. She hadn't tried to be unreasonable during their confrontation a few months ago, whatever Lucas might have thought. Was asking someone to be prompt and to keep his mind on his job so unreasonable?

Well, she didn't really have her mind on the job right now either.

"Don't worry about it." She fastened the buttons on her cardigan to keep from having to hold onto it and drew herself upright. "I'm sure, if we both remain professional, we'll come off this rotation relatively unscathed."

He gave her a dubious-looking smile. "I'm sure we will."

As he strode away, his glance cutting back to the chart and giving a shake of his head that could only be described as resigned, she realized that was the problem. Neither of them seemed able to maintain a calm professionalism around the other.

Two fortnights. That's all it was. Just because her rota corresponded with his, it didn't mean she had to stick to his side like glue. She could do this.

Doubt, like a whisper of smoke that curled round and round until it encased its victim, made her wonder if her ex-fiancé's cutting words were the hardest things she would ever face. She'd thought so at one time.

But as Lucas ducked around a corner and out of sight, she had a terrible suspicion she could be facing something much worse.

CHAPTER ONE

Present day

"CORA? WHAT'S WRONG, sweetheart?"

Lucas leaned a shoulder against the wall outside the birthing suite as his niece's voice came over the phone, dread making his blood pressure rise in steady increments. Every time he thought his brother was through the worst of his grief, he'd go on yet another binge and undo all the work he'd accomplished during therapy.

He took a quick glance down the hall. The coast was clear.

Lucas had worked hard over the last week to make sure his personal life didn't interfere with his job. As angry as he'd been at Darcie for giving him a public flogging over being late for work a couple of months ago, she'd been right.

It was why he'd hired a childminder to help with Cora's care. Burning the candle at both ends was not only unwise, it could also be dangerous for his patients.

Had his parents still been alive, they would have been happy to help. But it had been almost ten years since the car accident that had taken their lives.

His niece's voice came through. "Nothing's wrong. I just called to tell you what Pete the Geek did today."

Cora's Belgian sheepdog. Muscles he hadn't been aware he'd contracted released all at once. "Can you tell me later, gorgeous? I'm working right now."

"Oh, okay. Sorry, Uncle Luke. Are you coming for dinner tonight?"

"I wouldn't miss it, sweetheart." He smiled, unable to resist the pleading note in her voice. "What are we having?"

"Prawns!"

Cora's birth was what had propelled him to

change his career path from plastic surgery to midwifery. The lure of a glamorous life filled with beautiful women had faded away in a moment when Felix's wife had gone into labor unexpectedly. Lucas had delivered his own niece in the living room of his brother's home. As he'd stared down at the tiny creature nestled in his hands, Cora had blinked against the light and given a sharp wail of protest that had melted his heart. Seven years later, she still had the power to turn him into a soppy puddle of goo, especially since he and Felix were now the only family she had left.

He needed to get off the phone, but the ward was quiet—none of his patients were laboring at the moment. He cradled the device closer to his ear. "Prawns, eh? What's the occasion?"

She giggled. "Just because."

"You're going to spoil me." His chest tightened at how happy she sounded. He'd take this over those *other* phone calls any day.

"Oh," his niece said, "make sure you bring

some briquettes for the barbie. Daddy forgot them at the store."

Felix had forgotten quite a few things lately. But at least he seemed to be pulling out of his current well of depression.

Footsteps sounded somewhere behind him, so he moved to end the conversation.

"Okay, Cora, I will. Looking forward to tonight."

"Me too. Love you bunches."

"Love you even more, sweetheart. Bye." He ended the call, only to have the very person he'd been hoping not to encounter stalk past him, throwing an icy glare his way.

Lucas sighed. The woman did seem to pop up at just the wrong time. He slid the phone into his pocket and decided to go after her. He had no idea why, but he liked trying to get a rise out of her. Within five steps he'd caught up with her. Matching her pace, he glanced to the side.

Not good. The obstetrician's lips were pressed together into a thin line, her expression stony.

He pushed forward anyway, throwing her what he hoped was a charming smile. "Were you looking for me?"

Her expression didn't budge. "I was, but I can see you're busy."

"Just taking a short breather between patients. What was it you wanted?"

She glanced at him, her eyes meeting his for a mere second. "Is Isla scheduled to see you this week?"

Isla Delamere was one of his colleagues as well as a friend.

"Yes, did you want to be there for her appointment?"

Her chin edged up in a way he was coming to recognize. "I'd planned to be. She's my patient as well."

Okay, he'd gotten a rise out of her, but not quite the kind he'd been hoping for.

He moved ahead of her and planted himself in her path before she could reach the door to the staff lounge. Why he was bothering he had no idea, but something in him wanted to knock down a block or two of that icy wall she surrounded herself with. "Listen, Dr. Green—Darcie—I know we got off on the wrong foot somehow, but can we hit the reset button? We have three weeks of our rotation left. I'd like to make them pleasant ones, if at all possible. What do you say?"

The tight lines in her face held firm for another moment, and he wondered if she was going to strike him dead for daring to use her first name. Then her eyes closed, and she took a deep breath. "I think I might be able to manage that." The corners of her mouth edged up, creating cute little crinkles at the outer edges of her eyes. "If we both try very hard."

Something in Lucas's chest shifted, and a tightening sensation speared through his gut. Had he ever seen the woman smile? Not that he could remember, and certainly never at him. The transformation in her face was…

Incredible.

He swallowed. That was something he was better off not thinking about.

Three weeks. He just had to get through the rest of this rotation. From what he understood, Dr. Green had only been seconded to MMU for a year, then she'd head back to England. He did some quick calculations. She had, what…three months left? Once their rotation was over she'd be down to two, which meant it was doubtful they'd be paired together again. He gave an internal fist pump, trying to put his whole heart into it. It came off as less than enthusiastic.

Because you still have these three weeks to get through.

He gave her another smile. "I think I can manage it as well."

"Well, good. Now that that's settled, when is Isla's appointment?"

He checked his schedule. "Next Wednesday at two."

Darcie pulled her phone out and scrolled through a couple of screens before punching some buttons. "I don't have anyone scheduled at that time, so I'll be there." She gave him another smile—a bit wider this time—and the wobble in his chest returned. And this time he noticed the crinkles framed eyes that were green. A rich velvety color. Sparkling with life.

Her lips were softer too than they had been earlier. Pink, delicate, and with just a hint of shine.

The tightening sensation spread lower, edging beneath his waistband.

What the hell? Time to get out of here.

"Great. See you later." He turned and started back the way he had come, only to have her voice interrupt him.

"Don't forget to call for a consult if anything unusual comes up."

He stiffened at the prim tone. "Yes, I know the protocol, thank you."

When she didn't respond, he turned around and caught something…hurt?…in the depths of those green eyes, and maybe even a hint of uncertainty. In a flash, though, it winked out, taking with it any trace of her earlier smile and, very possibly, their newborn peace accord.

While that bothered him on a professional level, it was what he'd seen in her expression in that unguarded moment that made him want to cross over to her and try to understand what was going on in her head. He didn't. Instead, he chose to reiterate his comment in a less defensive way. "I'll ring if I need you."

Then he walked away. Without looking back. Praying the next weeks sped by without him having to make that call.

That man should wear a lab coat. A long one.

Darcie tried not to stare at the taut backside encased in dark jeans as he made his way back down the hall, but it was hard. No matter how much she tried to look anywhere but there, her peripheral vision was still very much engaged, keeping track of him until he finally turned down a neighboring corridor.

The thread of hurt from his curt response still

lingered, just waiting for her to tug on it and draw it tighter. Why had he acted so put out to have her assistance on a case?

Was it the professional rivalry that sometimes went on between midwives and obstetricians?

She sagged against the wall, pressing her fingers against her temples and rubbing in slow, careful circles to ward off the migraine that was beginning to chomp at the wall of her composure.

What was it about Lucas that put her on edge?

The fact that he was a man in a field dominated by women?

Or was it the fact that all the expectant mums who came through the doors clamored to be put on his patient list? Despite the run-ins they'd had over the past nine months, Senior Midwife Lucas seemed quite capable of doing his job with an ease and efficiency that only enhanced his good looks.

And they were good.

She tried to dredge up an unflattering image, like the time he'd come in late for work, dragging his fingers through his wavy hair, his rumpled clothes the same ones he'd had on when he'd left the previous afternoon. Nope. He'd been just as attractive then as the first time she'd laid eyes on him.

Ugh. She disliked him for that most of all.

Or maybe it was all those secretive phone calls she'd caught him making when he'd thought he'd been alone. Oh, those were definitely over the top. So many of them, right in the middle of his shift.

And he wondered why she was outraged when he came in late or took little side breaks to indulge in whispered conversations.

Could she be jealous?

She straightened in a flash. *No!* Just because Robert had decided she wasn't enough "fun", it didn't mean she should go ballistic over any man who wanted to indulge in a bit of pillow talk on the phone.

Maybe it wouldn't bother her so much if he didn't use the same flirty tones when in conversation with the MMU staff and his patients. The tone he turned on this "Cora" person—a kind of I'm-not-willing-to-commit-but-I-still-want-you-at-my-beck-and-call attitude that grated on Darcie's nerves. Especially after the way her ex had led her down the rosy path, only to dump her for her maid of honor—who, actually, *was* a lot of fun to be with.

She sighed and went into the lounge to get a strong cuppa that she hoped would relieve the steady ache in her head and keep it from blooming into something worse.

As soon as she moved into the space, she knew it was a mistake. Lucas, it seemed, was the main topic of conversation among the cluster of four nurses inside.

"I swear one of his patients this morning had on false eyelashes. While in labor!" Marison Daniels blinked rapidly, as if trying to imitate what the woman had done. They all laughed.

If Darcie had hoped to slide by them, grab her tea and tiptoe back out of the room unseen, that hope was dashed when the nurse next to Marison caught Darcie's eye and gave the jokester a quick poke in the ribs with her elbow. The laughter ceased instantly.

Oh, Lord. Her face burned hotter than the kettle she'd just switched on.

"Sorry. Didn't mean to interrupt."

"You didn't interrupt," Marison assured her. "I was just headed back to the ward."

The others all echoed the same thing.

With a scurry of feet and tossing of rubbish, the four headed out.

Just what she needed. To be reminded that she was still very much an outsider when it came to certain things—like being allowed to let her hair down with the rest of them.

No, the pattern had been set from the moment she'd got off the plane. Oh, she'd made friends and people were nice enough, but to let her in on their little jokes? That didn't happen very often, except with Isla.

Worse, she'd even overheard Lucas making fun

of her English accent while on one of his phone calls to Cora. It hadn't been in a mean way, he'd just repeated some of her colloquialisms with a chuckle, but it made her feel self-conscious any time she opened her mouth around him. So she made sure she spoke to him as little as possible. And now that they were sharing a rota, she was still struggling to maintain that silence.

Not that it was going to be possible forever.

She could still picture the confident way he strode through the hallways of the ward, his quick smile making itself known whenever he met a patient. She wrinkled her nose. More than one expectant mum would have probably given her left ovary to bat long sexy lashes and claim the child she was carrying was Lucas Elliot's.

Including his current paramour, Cora?

Probably, but not *her*. She was done with men like him.

Her fiancé had been handsome and attentive. Until he hadn't been. Until he'd grown more and more distracted as their engagement had progressed.

Now she knew why.

And Lucas had Cora. She was not about to smile and flirt with a man who was taken. She wasn't Tabitha.

She packed leaves into the tea ball and dropped it into a chunky mug—a gift from her dad to remind her that her favorite footballers resided in England and to not let herself get swept away by a handsome face, especially one who lived halfway round the world.

Lucas's quirked brow swam before her eyes, and she let out an audible groan, even as she poured boiling water into her cup. No matter how good looking he was or how elated she'd been to see the momentary confusion cross his expression when she'd smiled at him, she did not need to become like False-Eyelash Lady—the one Marison had carried on about.

There'd be a real corker of a reaction if someone caught her mooning after him. Or staring after him, like she'd done earlier.

She bounced her tea ball in the water and watched as the brew grew darker and darker, just like her thoughts. What she needed was to stay clearheaded. Like he'd said, they had three more weeks together.

He wanted them to be pleasant ones. She finished adding milk and sugar to her cup and then discarded the used tea leaves, rinsing the ball and leaving it on a towel for the next person who needed it.

"Pleasant" she could do, but that had to be the extent of it. Maybe she should be grateful for all those calls to Cora…maybe she should even hope the relationship stayed the course. At least for the next few weeks.

Which meant she would not go out of her way to put him at ease or cut him any slack if he came in late again. Neither would she give the man any reason to look at her with anything other than the casual curiosity his eyes normally held.

And once those three weeks were up?

Life would go back to the way it had been before they'd found themselves joined at the hip.

Joined at the hip. She gave a quick grin. That was one place she and Lucas would never be joined, even if the idea did create a layer of warmth in her belly. But it was not going to happen. Not in this lifetime.

With that in mind, she took a few more sips of the sweet milky brew, then, feeling fortified and ready to face whatever was out there, she headed off to see her next patient in what was proving to be a very interesting morning.

CHAPTER TWO

FELIX WASN'T AT HOME.

Arms loaded with items for their dinner, Lucas set everything down in the kitchen. "Where is he?"

Chessa, the childminder, shrugged and said in a quiet voice, "He went out an hour ago, saying he needed to buy prawns, and hasn't come back yet."

Damn. "And where's Cora?"

"Outside with Pete." The young woman's brow creased. "Should I be worried? He's been good for the last few weeks, but he did put some bottles of ale in the fridge. I haven't seen him drink anything, though."

"It's okay. It's not your job to watch him. If he ever fails to come home before you're supposed to leave, though, call me so I can make sure Cora is taken care of."

"I would never leave her by herself, Mr. Elliot." The twenty-five-year-old looked horrified.

"I know you wouldn't. I just don't want you to feel you have to stay past your normal time."

The sliding door opened and in bounded Pete the Geek in a flash of brown and white fur, followed closely by Cora, whose red face said they'd been involved in some sort of running game. The dog came over and sat in front of him, giving a quick woof.

Lucas laughed and reached in his pocket for a treat. "Well, you're learning."

He and Cora had been working on teaching Pete not to leap on people who walked through the door. By training him to sit quietly in front of visitors, they forestalled any muddy paw prints or getting knocked down and held prisoner by an overactive tongue. The trick seemed to be working, although if the tail swishing madly across the tile floor was any indication, Pete was holding himself in check with all his might.

Kind of like *him* when Darcie had smiled at him as he'd left the hospital?

Good thing he had more impulse control than Cora's dog.

Or maybe Darcie was training him as adeptly as Cora seemed to be training Pete.

"He wants his treat, Uncle Luke."

Realizing he'd been standing there like an idiot, he tossed the bacon-flavored bit to Pete and then bent down to pet him. "I think he's gained ten kilos in the last week."

He squatted and put an arm around both his niece and her dog.

Cora kissed him on the cheek, her thin arms squeezing his neck. "That's just silly. He doesn't weigh that much."

"No?" He gave her a quick peck on the forehead, grimacing when Pete gave his own version of a kiss, swiping across his eyebrow and half his eye in the process. "Okay, enough already."

He couldn't hold back his smile, however, despite the niggle of worry that was still rolling around inside him.

Where the hell was his brother?

Standing, he kept one hand on Pete's head and smiled at the minder. "Would you try ringing his mobile phone and seeing how long he'll be while I fire up the barbie and get it ready? I don't know about everyone else but I'm starving."

His voice was light, but his heart weighed more than the dog at his feet.

"Of course," Chessa said. "I'll bring you some lemonade in a few minutes."

As he was preparing the grill, she came out with a glass and an apologetic shake of her head. "There was no answer, but I left a voice mail."

"Thank you. Luckily I brought some prawns with me, just in case. Feel free to stay and eat with us, if you'd like."

She smiled. "Thanks, but if it's all the same to you, I think I'll head back to my flat. Do you need anything else?"

"No, I think we're good."

Twenty minutes later he had the briquettes going while Cora and Pete—worn out from a rough-and-tumble game of tug of war—lounged in a hammock strung between two gum trees, the dog's chin propped on his niece's shoulder. Both looked utterly content. Rescuing Pete had been the best thing his brother had ever done for his daughter, unlike a lot of other things since his wife's tragic death. In fact, the last four years had been a roller coaster consisting of more lows than highs—with the plunges occurring at lightning speed.

He went in and grabbed the package of prawns and some veggies to roast. Just as he started rinsing the shellfish, the front door opened and in came his brother. Bleary, red-rimmed eyes gave him away.

Perfect. Lucas already knew this routine by heart.

"Was our cookout tonight?" his brother asked, hands as empty as Lucas's stomach. "I forgot."

His molars ground against each other as he struggled with his anger and frustration. Was this what love and marriage ultimately led to? Forgetting that anyone else existed outside your own emotional state? Felix had a daughter who needed him, for God's sake. What was it going to take to make him look at someone besides himself? "Cora didn't forget."

His brother groaned out loud then mumbled, "Sorry."

"I'm just getting ready to throw it all on the barbie, so why don't you get yourself cleaned up before you go out there to see?"

The first two steps looked steady enough, but the next one swayed a bit to the left before Felix caught himself.

"Tell me you're not drunk."

"I'm not."

"Can you make it to your bedroom on your own?" The last thing Lucas wanted was for Cora to come in and see her father like this, not that she hadn't in the past. Many times.

Felix scowled. "Of course I can." He proceeded to weave his way down the hallway, before disappearing into one of the rooms—the bathroom.

Looks like you're spending the night on your brother's couch once again, mate.

Lucas had impressed on Cora the need to call him if her father ever seemed "not himself." The pattern was bizarre with periods of complete normalcy followed by bouts of depression, sometimes mixed with drinking. Not a good combination for someone taking anti-depressant medication.

He made a mental note to ask Felix if he was still taking his pills, and another note to make sure he arrived at work…on time! As he'd found out, it was tricky getting Cora off to school and then making the trek to the hospital, but if the traffic co-operated it could be done.

Otherwise that hard-won peace treaty would be shredded between pale English fingers.

Strangely, he didn't want that. Didn't want to disappoint her after he'd worked so hard to turn things around between them. Didn't want to lose those rare smiles in the process. So yes. He would do his damnedest to get to the hospital on time.

And between now and then he'd have to figure out what to do about his brother. Threaten him with another stint in rehab? Take away his car keys?

He cast his eyes up to the ceiling, trying not to blame Melody for allowing his brother to twine his life so completely around hers that he had trouble functioning now that she was gone.

Lucas never wanted to be in a position like that. And so far he hadn't. He'd played the field far and wide, but he still lived by two hard and fast rules: no married women and no long-term relationships. As long as he could untangle himself with ease the next day, he was happy. And he stuck to women who felt the same way. No hurt feelings. And definitely no burning need to hang around and buy a house with a garden.

Finishing up the veggies, he faintly caught the sound of the shower switching on, the *poof* from the on-demand water heater confirming his thoughts. Good. At least Felix was doing something productive. He opened the refrigerator, pulled out the ale in the door and popped the top on every single bottle. Then he took a long gulp of the one in his hand, before proceeding to pour the rest of the contents down the drain, doing the same with every other bottle and then placing the lot in the recycle bin. If the beer wasn't here, Felix couldn't drink it, right?

Not that that stopped him from going out to the nearest pub, but at least that took some effort, which he hoped Felix didn't have in him tonight.

Lucas went outside and loaded the prawns into a cooking basket and set it over the fire, then arranged the vegetables next to them on the grate. Cora's empty glass of lemonade was next to his full one. She was still sprawled on the hammock and it looked like both she and Pete were out for the count. If only he could brush off his cares that easily, he might actually get a full night's sleep.

But maybe tonight would be different. He'd

learned from experience that the fold-out cot in the spare room was supremely uncomfortable. He was better off just throwing a quilt over Melody's prized couch and settling in for the night there.

And he would wake up on time. He absolutely would.

And he'd arrive at work chipper and ready to face the day.

He hoped.

Something was wrong with Lucas.

He'd come through the doors of the MMU with a frown that could have swallowed most of Melbourne. She'd arrived at work armed with a smile, only to have him look right past her as if she didn't exist.

Ha! Evidently she'd been wrong about his reaction. Because there was nothing remotely resembling attraction in the man's eyes today. In fact, his whole frame oozed exhaustion, as did the two nicks on the left side of his strong jaw. He'd muttered something that might have been

"G'day." Or it might just as easily have been "Go to hell."

She was tempted to chase him down and ask about his evening, but when she turned to do so, she noticed that the back of his shirt was wrinkled as if he'd... Her gaze skimmed down and caught the same dark jeans he'd worn yesterday.

Her stomach rolled to the side. The staff all had lockers, and the last time he'd come in like this he'd used the hospital's shower and changed into clean clothes. That's probably what he was headed to do right now.

The evidence pointed to one thing. That he'd spent the night with "Cora" or some other woman.

The trickle of attraction froze in her veins.

None of your business, Darcie.

Just leave the man alone. If she made an issue of this, they would be back where they'd started: fighting a cold war that neither one of them would win.

But why the hell couldn't he drag himself out

of his lover's bed in time to go home and shower before coming to work?

Unless he just couldn't manage to tear himself away from her.

An image emerged from the haze that she did her best to block. Too late. There it was, and there was no way to send it back again—the one of Lucas swinging his feet over the side of the mattress, only to have some faceless woman graze long, ruby fingernails down his arm and whisper something that made him change his mind.

She shook her head to remove the picture and forced herself to get back to work.

Just as she did so she spied one of her patients leaning against the wall, her hands gripping her swollen belly. Margie Terrington, an English transplant like herself, had just come in yesterday for a quick check to make sure things were on track. They had been.

At least until now. From the concentration on her face and the grey cast to her skin, something wasn't right. Darcie glanced around for a nurse, but they were still tending to the morning's patients. Darcie hurried over.

"Margie? Are you all right?"

Her eyes came up. "My stomach. It's cramping. I think it's the baby."

"Let's get you into a room."

Alarm filled her. No time to check her in or do any of the preliminaries. This was the young woman's second pregnancy. She'd miscarried her first a little over a year ago, and she was only seven months along with this one. Too soon. The human body didn't just go into labor this early unless there was a problem.

Her apprehension grew, and she sent up a quick prayer.

Propping her shoulder beneath Margie's arm, they headed to the nearest exam room. One of the nurses came out of a room across the hall, and Darcie called out to her. "Tessa, could you come here?"

The nurse hurried over and got on the other side of their patient.

"Once I get her settled, can you see if you can find Lucas? He arrived a few minutes ago, so he might be in the lounge or the locker area. Let him know I might need his help."

"Of course."

The patient was sweating profusely—Darcie could feel the moisture through the woman's light maternity top. Another strike against her. If she had some kind of systemic infection, could it have crossed the placenta and affected the baby? A thousand possibilities ran through her mind.

Pushing into the exam area, the trio paused when Margie groaned and doubled over even more. "Oh, God. Hurts."

"Do they feel like contractions? Are they regular?" They finally got her to the bed and helped her up on it.

"I don't know."

Tessa scurried around, getting her vitals, while Darcie tried to get some more information. What she learned wasn't good. Margie had got up and showered like normal and had felt fine. Forty minutes later she'd got a painful cramp in her side—like the kind you got while running, she'd said. The pain had grown worse and had spread in a band across her abdomen. Now she was feeling nauseous, whether from the pain or something else, she wasn't sure. "And my joints hurt, as if I'm getting the flu."

Could she be?

As soon as Tessa called out the readings, the nurse went out to get the patient's chart and to hunt down Lucas.

"Let's get you into a robe and see what's going on."

"Wait." Margie groaned again. "I think I'm going to be sick."

Grabbing a basin, she held it under her patient's mouth as she heaved. Nothing came up, though.

"Did you eat breakfast?" Darcie started to reach for a paper towel, only to have Lucas arrive, chart in hand. He took one look at the scene and anticipated what she was doing. Ripping a couple of towels from the dispenser, he glanced at her in question. "What've you got?"

"This is Margie Terrington from Southbank. She's cramping. Pain in the joints. Nausea."

"Contractions?"

"I'm not sure. I'm just getting ready to hook her up to the monitor."

He tilted his head. "Theories?"

"None." She laid a hand on the young woman's shoulder. "Are you up to telling Lucas what you told me?"

Even as she asked it, Margie's face tightened up in a pained grimace, and she gave a couple of sustained breaths, dragging air in through her nose and letting it out through her mouth. A second or two later she nodded. "Like I told you, I took a shower this morning. Then I started getting these weird sensations in my side."

"What kind of weird?"

"Like a pulled muscle or something." She stiffened once again. She gritted out, "But now my whole stomach hurts."

"Where's the father?" Lucas asked.

"He's at work. I—I didn't want to worry him if it's nothing."

Lucas frowned. "I think he should be here." He glanced at Darcie. "Can you get her hooked up while I ring him?"

If anything, Margie looked even more frightened. "Am I going to lose this baby too?"

Darcie's heart ached for the woman, even as her brain still whirled, trying to figure out what was going on. "Let us do the worrying, love, can you do that?"

"I think so." She wrote her husband's phone number on a sheet of paper and handed it to Lucas.

While he was gone, Darcie got Margie into a hospital gown and snapped on a pair of gloves. Then she wrapped the monitor around her patient's abdomen. Wow, she was really perspiring. So much so that it had already soaked through the robe on her right side.

And her abdominal muscles were tight to the touch. "Are you having a contraction right now?"

Margie moaned. "I don't know."

She started up the machine and the first thing she heard was the quick *woompa-woompa-woompa-woompa* of the baby's heart. Thank God. Even as that thought hit, a hundred more swept past it. A heartbeat didn't mean Margie's baby wasn't in distress, just that he was alive.

She stared at the line below the heart rate that should be showing the marked rise and fall of the uterus as it contracted and released. It was a steady line.

Placing her hand on Margie's abdomen again, she noted the strange tightness she'd felt before. But it seemed more like surface muscles to Darcie. Not the deep, purposeful contraction of a woman's uterus.

Lucas came back and glanced at the monitor. "Your husband's on his way."

"Thank you." Another moan, and her hands went back to her stomach.

Lucas sat next to the bed and held the patient's hand, helping guide her through the deep breathing.

"She's not contracting." Darcie's eyes were locked on the monitor where a series of little squiggles indicated that something was happening, but it was more like a series of muscle fasciculations than the steady rise and fall she would expect to see. Could she have flu, like Margie suspected?

"When did you start sweating like this?"

Lucas's voice drew her attention back. He eased Margie's robe to the side and stared at the area where moisture was already beading up despite just having been exposed to the chilly air of the ward. Strange. Although Margie was perspiring everywhere—Darcie gave a quick glance at her face and chest above the gown—there was a marked difference between her moist upper lip and her right side, where a rivulet of liquid peaked and then ran down the woman's swollen belly.

"I don't know. An hour after my shower? Right about the time I started to hurt."

He peered at her closer. "You said you took a shower. Did you feel anything before or after it? A sting...or a prick maybe?"

A prick? Darcie stared at him, trying to figure out where he was going with this.

"No."

"Where did the pain start exactly?"

Margie pressed her fingers right over the area that was wet from perspiration.

He muttered something under his breath then glanced up at Darcie. "I need to make a quick phone call."

"What?" Outrage gathered in her chest and built into a froth that threatened to explode. Surely he was not going to make a personal call right now.

As if he saw something in her face, he reached out and encircled her wrist. "I want her husband to check on something at the house before he comes here," he said in a low voice.

The anger flooding her system disappeared in a whoosh as she stared back at him.

Margie's panicked voice broke between them. "What's wrong?"

"I'm not sure yet. But I don't think you're in labor."

"Then what?"

"I think you may have been bitten by a red-back," Lucas said.

"A what?" Margie asked.

"It's one of our most famous residents," he said. "It's a spider. A nasty one at that."

A redback! Darcie had heard of them but had never encountered one, and since she wasn't from Australia, it had never dawned on her that Margie could have been envenomed by something. Her patient was also from England. She'd probably never thought of that possibility either.

She glanced at Lucas. "Are they that common?"

"Quite." He patted Margie's hand. "If that's the case we have antivenin we can give you, which should help."

"If it is a bite, will it hurt the baby?" She gritted her teeth and pulled in another deep breath.

"I think we've caught it at an early stage." His gaze went back to the monitor, which Darcie noted still held steady. "I want to have your husband check the towel and your bathroom."

The patient's eyes widened. "I used the walk-in shower in the guest bathroom this morning. I almost never use that one because it's quite a long way from the bedroom. But my mother is due to fly in to help with the house and baby in a few weeks, and I thought I could tidy things and scrub the shower stall down as I was bathing."

"I'm just going to pull Dr. Green into the hall-way for a moment. I'll send the nurse in to sit with you."

Once they were outside the room, and Lucas had rung the husband, asking him to shake out the towel and examine the bathroom, she spun toward him. "A redback. Are you sure?"

"Pretty sure. Most Australians know what to look for, but no one else would. I've seen this once before. A redback bite that comes in look-ing like preterm labor."

She sagged against the wall. "God. I would have never checked for that. I didn't see a bite. Didn't even think to ask."

"You wouldn't have. And as for the bite mark..." He shrugged. "Small fangs, but they pack quite a wallop."

He gave a smile that looked as tired as she sud-denly felt.

"Can we give antivenin to her during preg-nancy?"

"We've given it before. I can't recall anyone having a bad reaction, unless the patient is aller-gic to the equine immunoglobulin in the serum." He sighed. "There've been some conflicting re-ports recently about whether or not the antivenin actually works, but I've seen enough evidence to tell me it's worth a shot. Especially since she's miscarried once already."

Lucas's mobile phone buzzed, and he glanced

at the screen. "It's him. Let's hope this is the answer we're looking for."

He punched a button asking a few questions before assuring the man that she should do well with the antivenin and telling him they'd be awaiting his arrival.

"He found the redback. It was still in the towel. A big one, from the sound of it." He dragged his fingers through his hair. "I'll need you to sign off on the medication. We'll go the intravenous route rather than administering the antivenin intramuscularly, since that's more favored at the moment."

"Of course." She closed her eyes with a relieved laugh. "God, I could kiss you right now. I never in a million years would have got that diagnosis right."

A few seconds of silence met her comment.

Hell. Had she really just said that? About kissing him?

Evidently, because when she dared to look at him again a thread of confused amusement seemed to play across his face. "I don't think now would be appropriate, do you, Dr. Green? But later…" He let his voice trail off in a way that gave her no question that he was definitely open to whatever later meant.

What? Hadn't he just come to work this morning all rumpled and sexed up?

Sexed up? Was that even a real expression?

Whether it was or not wasn't the point. It was unbelievable that he would roll out of one woman's bed and be ready and willing to kiss a second one. A perfect stranger, actually, since they barely knew each other.

Not likely, you jerk.

She gave the haughtiest toss of her chin she could manage and fixed him with a cold glare. "It's a figure of speech, Lucas, in case you haven't heard. I was just happy to know that Margie's symptoms have an explanation and a treatment. But get this straight. As grateful as I am for your help, I had no intention of *really* kissing you.

Now...or ever. I have no interest in being part of a love triangle. Been there. Done that."

Before she could scurry away in horror over that last blooper, he murmured, "I stand corrected on the kissing, although you totally had me for a moment or two. But I'm intrigued by this supposed love triangle you envision us in. Care to enlighten me as to who the third party might be, or do I have no say in the matter?"

Was he serious?

She wanted to hurl Cora's name at him. Instead, by some superhuman force of will, she clamped her jaws shut before they had a chance to issue any other crazy statements. Then, without another word, she swung back into their patient's room to give her the news about the redback.

At least he hadn't asked her about the been-there-done-that part of her rant, because no one needed to hear her sad tale about the wedding that almost had been. Or the woman who'd stolen her fiancé's heart when he was supposed to be madly in love with her.

Since when had she become so reckless with her words?

Just like the ruby stripe on the infamous redback that warned of dire consequences to those who came in contact with it, the answer to her last question was inscribed with words that were just as lethal: Lucas Elliot.

He made her forget about everything but his presence.

The thing was, she had no idea how to go about scrubbing him—or the image of their lips locking in a frenzy of need—from her mind and finishing out the rest of her time in Australia in relative peace.

But she'd better figure out an antivenin that would work against his charm and inject herself with it. As soon as she possibly could.

CHAPTER THREE

"How's Cora?"

Isla settled herself on the paper-lined exam table like a pro, despite the burgeoning evidence of her pregnancy.

A week after they'd successfully treated the redback spider victim, Darcie had somehow managed to keep her tongue to herself.

Ugh. Now, why did that thought sound so raunchy?

And why was it that every time she was around Lucas her mind hadn't quite stopped doing mental gymnastics over every word the man uttered, turning them over and over and looking for hidden meanings?

There weren't any, and he hadn't brought up the subjects of kissing, love triangles, or anything else of a personal nature, for which she was extremely grateful.

Here Isla was, though, bringing up the one person she had no desire to hear about.

Lucas's supposed lover.

As if hearing her thoughts, he glanced at her before looking back at their patient. "She's great. Wants me to buy her a sports car."

Darcie's eyebrows shot up, even though she tried to keep her facial features frozen into place. The woman had actually asked him to buy her a car? A pool of distaste gathered in the pit of her stomach. Just what kind of women did the man hang out with?

Isla, though, instead of castigating Lucas and telling him to kick the tramp to the curb, laughed as if she found that idea hilarious.

"Did you tell her she has to be tall enough to reach the pedals first?"

Her brain hit the rewind button and played those words over twice. Either he was dating a very short woman or...

"Yep. I also told her she has to be old enough to have her driving permit. So I'm safe for a few years."

Darcie couldn't help it. The words just came out. "Cora's not of legal age?"

"He hasn't talked your ear off about her yet? Wow." Her former flatmate blew out a breath. "She's his niece. And she gives him quite a bit of grief. Isn't that right, Lucas?"

The man in question studied Darcie as if he couldn't quite grasp something. "That's right, and…" The pupils in his eyes grew larger. "Oh, Darcie, I'm almost afraid to ask. Who did you think she was?"

"I—I…" She stammered around for a second then finally gave up.

He made a tutting sound then his lips curved. "I think I see. A love triangle, wasn't it? I don't know if I should be insulted or flattered."

"I just thought, she was—"

"My girlfriend?"

Isla's voice cut in. "Would someone like to

clue me in on what you two are going on about? What's this about a love triangle?"

"It's nothing."

Lucas spoke at the exact same time she did. He then laughed, while Darcie's face flamed.

Their patient looked from one to the other of them. "Oh, this is definitely *not* nothing. But…" she patted her belly "…someone is starting to use my bladder as his own personal football. So unless you want to take a break while I visit the loo, maybe we should get on with this."

"Of course." Lucas pulled out his measuring tape and stretched it over the bulge of Isla's belly, writing the results on her chart. "Right on schedule. At this rate I think the baby will weigh in at a little over seven pounds. The perfect size for a first baby."

"Thank goodness, because right now my stomach looks to be the size of a football." She gave a light laugh. "I guess that's why this little guy feels like he's training for the World Cup."

"Anything out of the ordinary? Contractions?"

"No. Nothing. I feel great." She glanced at Darcie. "Except I have to break our date for the beach this afternoon. Someone called off sick, and they've asked me to fill in."

"Don't worry about it. Some other time."

"I know, but I promised to take you to see some sights, and with everything with Alessi and the baby, time has just slipped away." Isla slid a look at Lucas. "Aren't you two on the same rota?"

A pit lodged in her stomach. "Yes, why?"

"Well, because…" She gave the midwife a wide smile. "Would you mind going in my place? Darcie and I were going to make a list of things for her to see and do. If she puts it off too much longer, she'll go back to England without having visited anything."

Her unease morphed into horror. "Isla, I'm sure he has other things to do with his off time than go to the beach."

"Actually, I'm free once our shift is over." The smile he gave her was much slower than Isla's and held a touch of challenge that made her shiver. "I'll be happy to help her make her list. And maybe even tick an item or two off of it. Since we *do* have the same rota. Unless she doesn't trust me, for some reason."

Isla skimmed her hands over her belly and gave a sigh that sounded relieved. "Of course she trusts you. That would be brilliant, Lucas. At this point, I would only slow her down."

They were making plans that she hadn't even agreed to. And go to the beach with Lucas? See those long legs stretched out on the sand beside hers? A dull roar sounded in her ears as panic set in.

"I'll be fine—"

A quick knock sounded before she could blurt out the rest of her sentence, that she would be fine on her own, that she didn't need company.

Sean Anderson, one of the other obstetricians, poked his head into the room. "Sorry, guys, they told me Isla was here." He looked at the patient, his expression unreadable. "One of your teen mums-to-be projects is at the nurses' station, asking for you. And after that your father wants to speak with you about your sister. I have a few questions about her myself."

Poor Isla. Not exactly the kind of thing one wanted to deal with when heavily pregnant.

Charles Delamere—Isla's father and the head of the Melbourne Victoria Hospital—had given her friend nothing but grief over her older sister's mad dash to England and the reasons behind it. Sean hadn't been far behind in the question department. But according to Isla, she'd promised Isabel that she would never reveal her secret to anyone. Especially not to Sean, since his coming to the hospital nine months ago had been what had sent Isabel running for the door in the first place.

She tried to avoid the other man's gaze as much as possible, until Isla sat up and grabbed her hand. "Would you come with me, since you wanted to know more about the teen mums program?"

Her eyes said it all. She didn't want to be alone

with Sean in case he grilled her again about Isabel. Darcie wouldn't have known about any of this except that Isabel's sudden departure had left an opening at both the MMU and in the Delameres' luxurious penthouse flat, which she'd shared with Isla until her friend's marriage to Alessandro.

Darcie had been all too happy to take Isabel's place, since she knew what it was like to run from something. In Darcie's case, it had been the right decision. In Isabel's, she wasn't so sure.

Isla hadn't told her much, but she knew Isabel was keeping something big from Sean. Maybe it was time for her to tell him the truth and see what happened.

But that wasn't her decision to make.

"Of course I'll come with you. It'll give me a chance to meet someone who's in the program."

As Isla threw her a grateful look and slid off the bed, Lucas, who'd been listening to their conversation without a word, wrapped his fingers around Darcie's wrist. "I'll meet you by the entrance after work. This'll give us a chance to discuss some things as well."

Like how she'd somehow managed to leap to the conclusion that his niece was some floozy that kept him out late at night and caused him to have a flippant attitude about work? Heavens, she'd misjudged the man, and she wasn't exactly sure how to make it right. But going to the beach with him was the last venue she would have chosen. For the life of her, though, she couldn't think of a way to get out of it. "If you're sure."

"More than sure." His thumb glided across the inside of her wrist, the touch so light she was almost positive she'd imagined it, if not for the cheeky grin that followed. Then he released her. "Give me a ring when you're done."

"'Kay."

Once out the door, she went with Sean and Isla to the waiting area, her shaking legs and thumping heart threatening to send her to the floor. It took several deep breaths to get hold of herself.

It turned out the expectant mum was there to

introduce Isla to a friend of hers—also a teen, also pregnant—who wanted to be included in the teen mums program. Darcie's heart ached over these young women who found themselves facing the unthinkable alone. She glanced at her friend, who greeted the newcomer with a smile, handing her a brochure that explained the enrolment process for TMTB. Darcie might not be able to understand what they went through, but Isla and Isabel understood all too well. Her chest grew tighter as she noticed Sean still standing behind them.

Oh, the tangled webs.

Once the girls were off on their way, Sean stepped forward. Holding up a hand, Isla stopped him in his tracks. "Don't ask, Sean. I can't tell you." She hesitated, and her mouth opened as if she was going to say something else then stopped.

All the heartache with Robert came rushing back, and Darcie realized how much simpler it would have been if he'd told her the truth when he'd first realized he loved someone else, rather than dragging out the process. If he hadn't kept his feelings for Tabitha a secret, maybe things would have been easier on all involved.

That thought propelled her next words.

"Maybe you should call Isabel and ask her yourself," she suggested, grabbing Isla's hand and giving it a quick squeeze of reassurance. She was half-afraid Isla would smack her for sticking her nose where it didn't belong.

Sean's blue eyes swung toward her. "I tried when I heard she was leaving, but she wouldn't take my calls."

Instead of cutting her off, Isla nodded, wrapping her arm around Darcie's as if needing to hold onto something. "Maybe, Sean…maybe you should just go there. If you're standing in front of her, she can't ignore you."

"Go to England?" he asked.

That was a fantastic idea.

Lucas had planted himself in Darcie's path a couple of weeks ago, and she'd been forced to stand there while he'd had his say. Maybe Sean should do the same. Once everything was out in the open, they could decide what to do with the truth. Or at least Isabel would be forced to tell him to his face that she wanted nothing to do with him. Somehow Darcie didn't think that's what the other woman would say when it came down to it. But, whatever happened, it was up to the two of them to hash things out. It wasn't Isla's responsibility, and she shouldn't have to act as intermediary, especially with a baby on the way. The last thing she needed was any added stress.

"I can give you her address, if you promise not to tell her where you got it," Isla added.

"My contract at the hospital *is* almost up." He dragged a hand through his hair, tousling the messy strands even more. "I'll have to think about it."

Isla's chin angled up a fraction of an inch. "I guess it comes down to whether or not you really want to know why she left, or how much you might come to regret it if you never take the chance and ask."

"I'll let you know if I need that address." With that, he strode down the hallway as if the very hounds of hell were hot on his heels.

Darcie sighed. "Do you think he will?"

"I don't know. Maybe the better question would be...if he *should*."

Why had he agreed to take her to the beach?

Lucas paused at the entrance to the car park to roll down the long sleeves of his shirt and button the cuffs against the cool air—or maybe he was gearing up for battle.

Having seen Darcie's face go pink when she'd realized Cora was his niece and not his lover had made something come to life inside him...as had her comment about a love triangle. The fact that she'd envisioned herself with him in that way was so at odds with how she'd always treated him that her flippant words had intrigued him. As had the thought of seeing her outside her own environment. Would the woman he'd come to view as an English rose—beautiful skin, green eyes, and a set of thorns that would pierce the toughest hide—turn into someone different once she stepped off hospital property?

That was why he'd agreed. If she was going to make any kind of transformation, he wanted to be there to see it.

He glanced back inside the hospital as he waited. It was spring in Melbourne, and the air definitely bore a hint of that as it had been warmer than usual. Hence Isla's suggestion of going to one of the beaches hadn't seemed too crazy. In fact, the temperature was still holding at almost nineteen degrees, and the sun was just starting to ease toward the horizon, so they wouldn't need jackets. Although in Melbourne that could change at any time.

"Hi, sorry I'm late," Darcie said in a breathless voice as the automatic doors closed behind her. "I wanted to grab a cardigan."

She'd done more than that. She'd changed from her dark trousers and white blouse into a long gauzy white skirt and a knit turquoise top that crossed over her chest in a way that drew attention to her full curves. Curves that made his mouth go dry.

The transformation begins.

He swallowed, trying to rid himself of the sensation. He'd expected her to let her hair down in a figurative sense. He hadn't expected to see those soft silky strands grazing the upper edges of her breasts.

That he was still staring at.

Forcing his eyes back to her face, where the color of her shirt made her eyes almost glow, he blinked back to reality. "Don't worry about it. Do you want to take the car or ride the tram?"

"Oh, the tram, please. I haven't ridden it to the beach yet, and it sounds like fun."

When he'd called the house, Chessa had said Felix was home and was grilling burgers on the barbie. When he'd tensely asked the childminder if he seemed "okay" she'd answered yes. For once he appeared clearheaded.

Thank God. The last thing he wanted to do

was skip out on his date with Darcie and ruin his reputation with her all over again.

Nope. This was not a date. Something he needed to remember.

"How do you usually get to the beach, then? Taxi?"

She glanced at him as they headed for the nearest tram station. "I haven't actually been yet. I hear they're beautiful."

"You haven't been to any of them?" Shock made him stop and look at her. Isla had mentioned taking her to see some sights, but surely she'd at least visited some of Melbourne's famed beaches.

"Nope. No time. That's why Isla suggested starting there and making a list of some other things."

They started walking again. Hell, she'd been here how long? Nine months? "Well, I'm glad she mentioned it, then. We can get a snack at one of the kiosks if you want. The beaches are prettier in the morning, though."

Maybe he should take her to see the sun rise over the ocean. Those first rays of light spilling onto the water and sand made them flash and glitter as if waking from a deep slumber.

Like him?

Of course not. He wasn't asleep. He was purposeful. Conscious of every move he made and careful to keep his heart far from anything that smacked of affection...or worse. He'd seen firsthand what had happened with Felix and Cora when Melody had died. He never wanted anyone to have to explain to a child of his the things he'd had to explain to his niece. That her father was very sad that her mother had gone away.

You mean she died.

Cora had said the words in her no-nonsense, too-adult-for-her-age manner that made his heart contract.

His niece needed him for who knew how long. He wouldn't do anything that would jeopardize his ability to be there for her.

Especially not for love.

That wasn't true. "Love" was exactly why he'd decided to remain single. He needed to expend all his emotional energy on a little girl who desperately needed a dependable, stable adult. Something that Felix couldn't be. At least not yet.

Buying their tickets, he eased them over to the queue, where a few people waited for the next tram to arrive.

Darcie's soft voice came through above the sound of nearby traffic. "I owe you an apology."

He glanced over in surprise to see her hands clasped in front of her, her eyes staring straight ahead. "For what?"

"For chastising you for being late all those months ago. I thought you were...that Cora was..." She shrugged.

The tram, with its bright splashes of color, pulled to a halt as he processed her words. They both got on and grabbed an overhead strap, since all the seats were full. As they did so, he suddenly saw the whole situation through Darcie's eyes. If she truly had thought his niece was a woman, then all those times he'd come rushing into work after sleeping on his brother's couch had to look pretty damning when viewed through that lens.

He stepped closer to prevent anyone from hearing and leaned down. "I should have explained, but I thought it was—"

"None of my business. And it wasn't. If I had questions, I should have asked you directly."

Whether the reasons had been valid or not, she'd been right in expecting him to be prompt and ready to work when it was time for his assigned shift. "I should have tried harder."

Except that sometimes there'd been no way to do that. He'd had to take Cora to school on mornings that Felix had been recovering from a bender or, worse, when he hadn't come home for the night. There'd been that worry on top of having to care for his niece. There had been days he probably shouldn't have come in to work at all. Except his sense of duty had forced him to march in there—late or not—and do what he'd promised to do.

After a while, though, all those promises had begun to bump into one another and fight for supremacy. His niece had to come first. And he would make no apologies for that.

The tram started up and Darcie lurched into him for a second. He reached out with his free hand to steady her, but she recovered, pulling away quickly and clearing her throat. "Does your niece live with you?"

His grip tightened slightly on the handhold, but he forced his voice to remain light. "She lives with my brother, but I help out with her every once in a while."

That was the understatement of the year. But he loved Cora. He'd give his life for her if he had to.

Sensing she was going to ask another question, he added. "Her mom died of cancer a few years ago."

She glanced up at him. "I'm so sorry, Lucas."

So was he. But that didn't change anything.

"Thank you." He braced himself to go around a curve, and Darcie—not anticipating the shift—bumped into him once again. This time the contact sent a jolt of awareness through him. He just prevented himself from anchoring her against him, and instead changed the subject. "So how is it that you haven't seen any of our beaches? As busy as you are, surely you could have managed one side trip."

"It's no fun on my own." She gestured at the sights outside the tram, which were racing by with occasional stops to pick up or let off passengers.

With Isla busy building her own life, Lucas had never stopped to wonder how Darcie was faring now that she had the Delamere flat all to herself. That made him feel even worse. "You should have asked someone at the hospital to go with you."

"It's okay. I understand how busy everyone is."

Their bodies connected once more, and this time he couldn't help but reach out to make sure she didn't stumble or hit the passenger on her other side. She didn't object, instead seeming to lean in to brace her shoulder against his chest. Or that could just be his damned imagination since the contact seemed to be burning a hole through his shirt. Whatever it was, he was in no hurry to let her go again. Except they were nearing the Port Melbourne Beach, which was one of the best locales for a newbie tourist. "Let's get off at this one."

When the tram stopped, he reached for her hand and guided her to the nearest door. Stepping down and waiting for her to do the same, he glanced around. "I want to get a notebook."

"What for?" she asked, brushing her skirt down her hips.

"To make that list Isla mentioned."

She reached into her bag and pulled out a small spiral-bound pad. "I have this if that would work."

"Perfect. We can sit down and put our heads together."

She paused then said, "Oh, um…sure, that

would be great. But you really don't have to go with me to see the city."

It was said with such a lack of enthusiasm that he smiled. "I told Isla I would. Besides, I want to. It'll be one way for me make amends."

"Are you sure? If anyone needs to make amends, it's me."

He allowed his smile to grow as he took the notepad from her and headed toward the paved footpath that led to the beach. "You were just trying to avoid that love triangle you mentioned."

Darcie laughed, a low throaty sound that went straight to his groin and lodged there. "For all I knew, it could have been a love hexagon...or octagon."

"Hmm, that might be a little ambitious even for someone like me."

"Someone who jumps from woman to woman?"

He shook his head. "Nope. I don't jump. I just don't stick around long enough to make any kind of angles—triangular or otherwise."

And if that didn't make him sound like a first-class jerk, he didn't know what did. "That didn't come out exactly right."

"It's okay. I understand. You're just not interested in serious relationships. Same here."

"Really? No serious relationships back in England?"

"Not at the moment."

"So there was someone?" The pull in his groin eased, but a few other muscles tensed in its place. Why did the idea of her being with someone else put him on edge?

"I was engaged. I'm not any more."

Those seven words were somehow more terrible than if she'd gone through a long convoluted explanation about why she and her fiancé had come to their senses and realized they weren't meant to be together. They spoke of heartbreak. And pain.

All the more reason for him to stay out of the dating pool.

"I'm sorry it didn't work out."

"Me too."

So she still loved the guy? She must. What the hell had her fiancé done to her?

He reached down and squeezed her hand, and instead of letting go he held on as they reached the wide footpath that ran along the far edge of the beach where other people strolled, jogged or rolled by on skates or bicycles.

"Wow, it's busy for so late in the afternoon," she said.

"It's a nice day. Do you want to walk in the sand or stick to the path?"

"Definitely the sand. Let me take my shoes off." Stepping to the side and grasping his hand more tightly, she kicked off one sandal and then the other, reaching down to pick them up and tuck them into the colorful tote bag she carried. "Your turn."

He let go of her hand long enough to remove his loafers and peel off his socks, shoving them into his shoes. He then tucked the notebook under his right arm so he could hold his shoes with the same hand.

Once their feet hit the sand their fingers laced back together as if by magic, and Darcie made no move to pull away.

She was a visitor. Alone, essentially, and dealing with a broken engagement. He was offering friendship. Nothing more.

And if she offered to drown her sorrows in his arms?

All the things that had gone soft suddenly headed back in the other direction.

Hell, Lucas, you've got to get a grip.

It might have been better if she'd never shown him her human side. Because it was doing a number on him. Okay, so he could show her some things. Maybe he'd invite Cora along for the ride. He could make sure his niece was being cared for and have a built-in chaperone should his libido decide to put in more appearances.

Darcie stopped halfway to the shoreline, her arm brushing his as she took in the sights around her.

"What's that ship?" She motioned to where the

Spirit was docked, waiting on its next round of travelers, its large sleek shape a normal part of the landscape here at the beach.

"It carries passengers and vehicles across to Tasmania. Maybe that's first thing we should put on your list."

"Maybe."

Darcie's hair flicked around her face in the breeze from the surf, the long strands looking warm and inviting in the fading rays of the sun. His fingers tightened around his shoes, trying to resist the urge to catch one of the locks to see if it was as silky as it appeared. Good thing both of his hands were occupied at the moment.

"It's lovely here," she murmured.

It was. And he wasn't even looking at the water. Why had he never noticed the way her nose tilted up at the end, or the way her chin had the slightest hint of an indentation? And the scent the wind tossed his way was feminine and mysterious, causing a pulling sensation that grew stronger by the second.

"I agree." He forced his eyes back to the shore-line and started walking again. "Are you hungry? We could grab something and sit on the sand. Then we could start on that list while we eat."

She reached up and pushed her hair off her face with her free hand. "That sounds good. I should have brought an elastic for my hair."

"I like it down."

Green eyes swung to meet his. She blinked a couple of times. "It's not very practical."

"Neither are a lot of things." Why was he suddenly spewing such nonsense? He motioned to a nearby vendor. "How about here?"

They bought some ice-cream bars and ate them as they strolled a little further down the beach. By the time they'd finished they'd come across an area that wasn't packed with people. "Can we stop?" she asked.

"I didn't think to bring a blanket."

"It's fine." Dropping her shoes and bag onto the soft sand, she sat cross-legged, covering her legs with her skirt. Then she propped her hands behind her hips and lifted her face to the sky. She released a quiet exhalation, a sound that spoke of letting go of tension…along with a hint of contentment.

She was still transforming—losing some of those hard, brittle edges she had at the hospital. Maybe they were simply a result of working long hours with little or no downtime. Because right now she was all soft and mellow, her billowing skirt and bare feet giving her a bohemian, artsy flare he'd never have equated with Dr. Darcie Green. And he liked it. The hair, the pale skin, the casual way she'd settled onto the sand, curved fingers burrowing into it. That firm behind that had bumped against him repeatedly as they'd ridden the tram.

The list! Think about something else. Anything else.

He opened the notebook and riffled through pages of notes from what must have been a medical seminar until he came to a blank sheet. He drew a pen from his shirt pocket. "So what would you like to see or do while in Australia?"

Her eyes blinked open but she didn't look at him. Instead, she stared out at Port Phillip Bay instead. "Mmm. Travel to Tasmania on that ship we saw?"

His pen poised over the paper as she paused for a second.

"Do some shopping. Visit a museum." Her brows knitted together as she thought. "See some of the parks. Go to a zoo."

She glanced his way, maybe noticing he wasn't writing. Because he was still too damn busy looking at her.

He shook himself. "Those are all safe things—things every tourist does. You should have at least one or two things that are a little more dangerous."

"Dangerous?" Her eyes widened just a touch.

"Not dangerous as in getting bitten by a redback but dangerous as in fun. Something you never would have done had you remained in

England. Something outrageous and wild." He leaned a little closer. "Something you'll probably never get a chance to do again."

There was silence for a few seconds then her gaze skimmed across his lips and then back up, her cheeks turning a luscious shade of pink.

Oh, hell. He was in deep trouble. Because if the most outrageous thing she could picture doing was pressing her mouth to his… Well, he could top that and add a few things that would knock her socks—and the rest of her clothes—right off.

"What are you thinking?"

She shook her head. "Nothing."

"Darcie." His voice came out low and gruff. "Look at me."

Her face slowly turned back toward him.

"If I write, 'Kiss a non-triangular Aussie' on this list, would you consider that wild and dangerous?"

There was a long pause.

"Yes," she whispered.

His gut spun sideways. He hoped to God he'd

heard what he thought he'd heard, because he was not backing away from this. His brain might have come to a standstill, but his body was racing forward at the speed of light.

He set the notebook on the sand, one hand coming up to cup her nape. "Do you want to tick at least one thing off that list before we leave this beach? Because you have a willing member of the male Aussie contingent sitting right next to you."

"You?"

"Me."

He reeled her in a little closer, his senses coming to life when her eyes slowly fluttered shut.

He would take that as a yes.

His body humming with anticipation, Lucas slowly moved in to seal the deal.

CHAPTER FOUR

HE TASTED LIKE ice cream.

Darcie wasn't quite sure how it happened, but that tram ride must have messed with her head, muddled her thinking, because somehow Lucas was kissing her, his mouth sliding over hers in light little passes that never quite went away.

That was good, because once the contact stopped the kiss would be over.

And that was the last thing she wanted.

There were people walking on the path not ten meters behind them, but it was as if she and Lucas were all alone with just the beach and the sound of the surf to keep them company.

His lips left hers, and she despaired, but he was back in less than a second, the angle changing, the pressure increasing just a fraction. Her arms started trembling from holding herself upright, and as if sensing her struggle he eased her down, hand beneath her head until she touched the sand.

The flavor of the kiss changed, going from what she feared might be a quick peck—the thing of friends or family members—to a full-on assault on her senses…a *kiss*.

If he was out to prove that Aussie men were hot-blooded, he'd done that. He'd more than done that. There was a raw quality to Lucas that she didn't understand but which she found she liked. As if he were a man on the edge—struggling to keep things casual but wanting, oh, so much more.

So did she.

Darcie opened her mouth.

The kiss stilled, and she wondered if she'd gone too far or if he was trying to process what to do at this point.

You said wild and dangerous. I'm laying myself open to it so, please, don't make me sorry.

He didn't. His tongue dipped just past her lips, sliding across the edge of her upper teeth before venturing further in. Her nerve endings all came to life at once, nipples tightening, gooseflesh rising on her arms.

Maybe she could tick that item off her list multiple times…right here, right now.

She wound her arms around his neck, reveling in the sense of urgency she now felt in his kiss. His free hand went to her waist and tightened on it, his thumb brushing across her ribs in a long slow stroke.

Then he withdrew, pulling back until he was an inch from her mouth.

"Damn." His curse brushed across her lips, but he didn't sound angry. Not like he had when he'd seen the rotation schedule. More like surprised.

He sat up, using the hand behind her head to help her up as well. "We'd better start actually making that list or it's never going to get done."

Who cared about some stupid list?

His jotting things down, though, gave her a chance to compose herself. Well, a little. Because nothing could have prepared her for that kiss. Not her relationship with Robert or any of her past dating experiences.

Lucas was… She wasn't sure what he was. But he was good.

She glanced over at the sheet of paper where he'd made a list of about ten things. "Kiss an Aussie" was first on the list, but the tick mark he'd made beside it was now scratched through.

"I thought we were going to cross that off."

The look he gave her was completely serious. "We can't tick something off a list that didn't exist at the time it happened."

"We can't?"

"No." His eyes went dark with intent. "Because if you want to experience a real Aussie kiss, it has to be behind closed doors—with no audience to distract you."

Distracted? Who'd been distracted? Certainly not her.

But if he wanted to kiss her again—like that—she was more than willing to play along.

He scrawled a couple more words.

"Hey, wait a minute. I never said I wanted to bungee jump."

"Dangerous, remember?"

"But—"

"I have a friend who used to have a bungee-jumping business. He closed it last year but still lets friends take a dive from time to time. And I promised Cora—my niece," he reminded her with a smile, "that she could come out and watch me do a jump."

It was her turn to be surprised. "You bungee jump?"

"I have to get my adrenaline pumping somehow, since I don't have any love triangles to keep me busy."

That was something she didn't even want to think about, because she might end up volunteering if she wasn't careful.

She wouldn't mind meeting his niece, though. And it wasn't like *she* had to jump.

"Okay, I'll go. But I don't promise I'm going to do anything but watch."

"Oh, no, gorgeous, you're going to do a whole lot more than that. I promise."

Why had he invited her on his and Cora's day out?

Because he'd been too strung out on kissing her two days ago to think clearly when he'd written that item on her so-called list. She and Cora had been chatting the whole trip, with Darcie twisted around in her seat in order to talk to her. Why couldn't Cora have hated her on sight?

But she hadn't. And her "Are you Uncle Luke's girlfriend?" had turned Darcie's face the color of pink fairy floss. She hadn't freaked out, though. She'd simply shaken her head and said that she was just a friend.

Huh. He couldn't remember any friends kissing him the way she had.

And it had shocked the hell out of him. Prim and proper Darcie Green had something burning just beneath the surface of those cool English features. He had the singe marks on his brain to prove it.

As they stood on the edge of the tower suspended over a deep pool of water, Cora bounced up and down with excitement but Darcie looked nervous. "You don't have to do this, you know," he murmured.

"Are you sure it's safe? What if…?" She nodded toward Cora.

He understood. What if something happened in front of his niece? And maybe it hadn't been the smartest thing to bring her up here to watch. But she'd been begging to watch him do one of his jumps for a while now.

"Max Laurel is an engineer and a friend." He glanced over at where a stick-straight figure was adjusting some fittings. "He has his PhD in physics. I trust him. And at a hundred feet the tower isn't very high. Even if the bungee-cord snaps, there's a safety line. If that fails as well, I'll just go into the water."

He gave her a quick smile. "Like I told you earlier, he only does it for friends, he's not open to the public any more."

"What happens when you finish the jump?"

"Max will lower me the rest of the way into the water, and I'll undo the cables and swim to the side." He understood her nerves, but compared to what had happened between them back at the beach this felt pretty tame. No way was he about to admit that to her, though.

Neither was he planning on being the Aussie she checked off her list, despite his words to that effect.

Strung out on kisses.

Yep, there was no better way to put it than that. But it had to stop now. Because he had a feeling things could get out of hand really quickly with Darcie for some reason. And not just for him. She'd just come out of a bad relationship and he didn't want her to get the idea that anything serious could come of them being tossed together at work and for a few outside excursions. He had enough on his plate with Felix and Cora to risk complicating his life any further.

"You ready, Luke?" his friend asked.

"I am. Can you hold on just a minute?"

Going down on his haunches in front of his niece, he put his hands on her shoulders. "Are you sure you're okay with this? I don't want you to be scared."

"No way! As soon as I'm old enough, I'm going to do it too."

Lucas had told her she had to wait until she was eighteen before attempting it. He wanted to make sure her bones and joints were strong enough to take the combination of her weight and the additional force that came from the jump. He smiled at her bravado, though. "Then let's get this show on the road."

"Darcie is going to jump too, isn't she?"

He glanced up at the woman in question. "Depends on how brave she's feeling."

"I'm only feeling half-brave. Is that enough?"

The fact that she was here, at the top of the

tower, said she was more than that. She could have backed out of the trip altogether and he wouldn't have stopped her. But here she was. "More than enough."

"I'll cheer you on," promised Cora. "I wish Daddy had come, though."

Lucas hadn't told Darcie why he helped so much with his niece, and he was glad to keep it that way. For Felix's sake.

His brother was supposed to be seeing his counsellor today. Lucas could only hope he was keeping his word. His behavior the other day seemed to have snapped him back to awareness. Then again, they'd been down that same road a couple of times.

So he settled for a half-truth. "I'm sure he'll come next time. He had some things he needed to do today."

When he glanced at Darcie a slight pucker formed between her brows before it smoothed away again.

Did she suspect things weren't quite right in the Elliot household? Time to shift her attention.

"Okay, Max, are you ready for me?"

"Just about."

The next several minutes were spent attaching a thick cable to his ankles and an additional safety line to a harness that went around his torso. If something happened to the first elastic band the second one was meant to catch him. He'd done this at least twenty times with no ill-effects. Then again, he'd never had his niece and a woman watching him go over the side. Something inside him poked at him to show off for Darcie—do a spectacular swan dive or something, but that was out of the question. Safety had to come first when it came to Cora.

He moved into position, and Max checked everything once again and then gave him the thumbs-up sign. Lucas counted to three in his head and then…

Over!

He catapulted out into the air, gravity pulling

him into a smooth arc as he began his downward trajectory.

The wind whistled in his ears, and he thought he might have heard Cora shout, but it was all lost in the exhilaration of the jump. Although, as the elastic began to grab and slow his descent, he wondered if even this could top that kiss he'd shared with Darcie.

Damn.

The bungee yanked him halfway back up before letting him fall again. But the closer he got to the end of his jump, the more irritated he became. This had once filled his senses like nothing else ever could. And where he'd been happy to share it with her a couple of days ago, he was now not so sure that he'd done the right thing.

His bouncing halted, but unfortunately his wavering thoughts kept right on careening up and down, the whine of the motor as Max slowly lowered him down to the water failing to drown them out for once. Then he hit the pool and let his buoyancy carry him back to the surface, where he unhooked himself from the bungees and ankle straps, and did a slow side crawl to the edge of the pool.

He looked up and saw two faces looking down at him. One filled with an elation he recognized from years of seeing that same expression. One filled with uncertainty, as if the woman he'd known for less than a year had sensed what had been in his head as he'd done the dive.

This was not her fault. It was his own damn exhaustion and worry about Felix catching up with him. It had to be that. It couldn't be that Darcie had somehow struck a chord inside him that was still reverberating two days later.

If it was…then somehow he had to figure out a way to silence whatever she'd started.

Lucas was in the water at the far side of the pool. Waiting for her to jump so he could help her unfasten the bungees. Max told her he'd set the tension so that she wouldn't drop as far as Lucas had before it caught her up. Then the winch would let out the line until she slid into the water. Piece of cake.

Easy for him to say. Lucas hadn't come up to give her a pep talk or anything. He'd remained at the bottom, radioing up from a walkie-talkie on the side of the pool that he'd stay down and help Darcie.

Maybe it was just as well that he hadn't come back up because everything on her body was trembling. Even her hair follicles seemed to be vibrating in terror. She wasn't afraid of heights, but something about jumping and hoping an elastic cord would somehow stop her from hurtling headfirst into the water was a scary prospect.

"You can do it, Darcie." Cora's cheerful voice broke into her thoughts.

Not willing to let the girl see how scared she was, she pasted on a smile she hoped looked halfway real. "You'll be okay up here?"

"Oh, yeah. I'm going to take pictures of you as you go over."

Perfect. Just what she needed. For this moment

HER PLAYBOY'S SECRET

to be recorded for all to see. She would have to find a discreet way to ask Max not to put it up on his wall of fame. Where Lucas's image appeared in several different sets of swim trunks his face was always filled with that same look of exultation, eyes closed as if taking in every second of the jump.

Speaking of jumps, she'd better go before someone got tired of waiting and pushed her over. "Okay, Cora. Count to three, and I'll jump."

"Woo-hoo!" The child yelled down to Lucas. "Get ready, here she comes. One…two…*three!*"

Darcie held her arms out from her sides and jumped as far away from the tower as she could, just as Max had instructed her. The fabric buckles of the ankle harness were where her every thought was centered right now, and she squeezed her eyes shut tight. She fell…and fell. Suddenly, she felt a firm tug that turned her so she was facing the water—at least she assumed so since she still couldn't bring herself to look. A squeal left her throat before she could stop it as she bounced several times, still with her head pointed straight down. Then she came to a halt.

Hanging. Upside down. In midair. Just like a bat.

She chanced a glance down and saw that Lucas was there, right below her. The sight of him made her pounding heart calm slightly as a mechanical hum sounded from the tower above her. Slowly, she started moving downward at a steady rate. Coming closer and closer to those familiar features.

His arms stretched up as she came within reach and he put a hand around her shoulders, keeping her from plunging headlong into the water. Her body made a curve before his other arm wrapped around her hips. He went under, still holding her. That's when she realized he was treading water and her weight was sending him down. She struggled to free herself, kicking with her legs to keep from drowning the man.

But he didn't come back up. Instead, she felt his hands on one of her ankles, and she stopped paddling to let him undo the carabiner that attached the bungee cord to her legs. She sank beneath the surface and opened her eyes. There he was, fingers undoing the shank that held her ankles together, before moving further up to unclasp the static safety line at her waist.

His eyes were open as well, and they looked into hers. He reached out to finger a strand of her hair that floated between them, making her exhale a stream of bubbles. Then he leaned forward and gave her a quick kiss before grabbing her hands and dragging her upward. A good thing, because suddenly she'd forgotten that she needed to breathe.

Once at the surface she dragged in a couple of ragged breaths while Lucas kept his arm around her waist and waited while she composed herself and prayed for her nerves to settle down just a bit.

"You did it."

"I can hardly believe I jumped." The elation was slow to kick in, but it was there now that she knew she was safely at ground level again.

"I can hardly believe it either." Lucas smiled and leaned in close to her ear. "Well, it looks like you got your first tick mark, Dr. Green. Congratulations."

Since she'd just jumped off a tower into the water, she assumed he was talking about the bungee-jumping item on the list they'd made together.

Which meant he wasn't counting that quick kiss in the water as having completed that other item on her list.

Because he was still waiting on the behind-closed-doors part to happen?

Oh, Lord. And she'd thought bungee-jumping was dangerous. It was tame compared to what her head conjured up.

The prospect of being with Lucas in a quiet, non-public place had to qualify as wild and outrageous, right? Because right now she couldn't imagine a scarier prospect than finding herself back in his arms.

CHAPTER FIVE

CORA WAS ASLEEP.

Glancing in the rearview mirror on the way back to the house, a shard of concern worked its way through his chest. He hadn't realized until after he'd helped Darcie from the pool that his niece had been taking pictures of their jumps. He wasn't quite sure what she'd been able to see from the tower, but he hoped that impulsive peck on the lips had been safely hidden beneath the water.

Why had he done that anyway? Kissed her. Again.

Because as he'd seen her sail toward him at the end of that bungee cord she had been so different from the person he'd imagined Darcie Green to be for the last nine and a half months. She'd seemed as free as a bird, tethered only by those safety cords. He'd halfway thought she'd back out of it once the time came. She hadn't.

He was happy for her in a way that was alien to him. And unsettling.

Maybe he should get some things straight with her. Only he didn't want to do that in front of his niece in case she wasn't really asleep.

"Do you mind if we drop Cora off first?"

"Of course not. But I can take a taxi if you want to just drop me off at the hospital."

"Your flat is on the way back, so it's not a problem. You're still at the Delamere place, right?" He'd been to the luxurious penthouse flat for a few parties thrown by Isla and Isabel.

"Yes, I'm there. Are you sure you don't mind?"

"Not at all." He glanced over at her, noting she'd gone back to her prim way of sitting with her hands clasped in her lap. "Did you have fun today?"

After he'd done a couple more jumps—Darcie demurring that once had been more than enough—they'd put on some dry clothes and had then had lunch with Max. That's when Cora had mentioned getting dozens of pictures and that she couldn't wait to show them to him and Darcie.

Showing them to him was one thing. But Darcie?

He was going to preview them first before that happened.

"I did, actually." Her eyes flicked to his and then back to the road in front of them. "I'll probably never get a chance to do anything like that again. Please, tell your friend thank you."

Darcie had already told him multiple times. In fact, she'd seemed to hang on his friend's every word during lunch. He'd been glad in a way, but watching her laugh over something Max had said had also caused a dark squirming of his innards he wouldn't quite call jealousy but it was something he didn't recognize. And didn't like.

"I noticed you exchanged social media information so you can do that."

She frowned and threw him a sharp glance.

"Should I not have? He was the one who initiated it."

Yes, he had. And the last thing he wanted was to risk Max's friendship over a woman who would be gone in a couple of months.

He settled for saying the first thing that came to mind. "Max's a nice guy. He doesn't have a lot of experience with women."

Oh, and that sounded awful. Darcie evidently agreed because a dark flush came to her cheeks. "I think it would be better to let me off at the hospital, if you don't mind."

Prim. Uptight. Formal. All things he associated with the Darcie of three months ago. Not the warm, open woman who'd accompanied him today.

He took his hand off the wheel and covered her twined fingers. "I didn't mean that as a cut, Darce. I know you wouldn't do anything to lead him on." Why he'd felt the need to shorten her name all of a sudden he had no idea. But he liked it. Liked the way it rolled off his tongue with ease.

Another reason it would be good to talk to her. Because she was a nice girl. Just like he'd talked about Max being a nice guy. He didn't want to do anything to lead *her* on. And those two kisses they'd shared could have definitely made her think things were headed down the wrong path.

Weren't they?

Absolutely not.

"You're right. I wouldn't lead him—or anyone else—on, or make them think things that weren't true."

The words were said with such conviction that Lucas glanced at her again and made an educated guess. "Your ex?"

"Yes." She paused for a moment. "Let's just say it's made me careful about how I interact with men."

Wow. Had that been part of those angry sparks that had lit up the maternity ward whenever he'd had dealings with her? He wasn't sure. But one thing he did know, he didn't want to go back to those days.

So maybe he should just cool the warning-her-off speech he'd planned. Wasn't he assuming a lot in thinking she was going to fall all over him because of his two lapses in judgment? Wasn't he being an egotistical jerk to think he was that irresistible?

Good thing the drive over to Felix's house gave him time to think before he did something else stupid.

Speaking of his brother's house… They were nearing the street. He put his hand back on the gear lever and downshifted as he turned at the corner. Five houses went by and they'd arrived.

Once in the driveway, he motioned for Darcie to wait while he got Cora out of the backseat. Unbuckling his niece and easing her from the car, he swung her up into his arms. She peered out of one eye then flicked it shut again.

"Cora, have you been pretending to sleep this whole time?"

"No." The word was mumbled, but there were guilty overtones to it.

Perfect. Good thing he'd decided not to tackle heavier subjects while driving.

And his comment about Max, and practically holding her hand a few minutes ago? Hopefully Cora's eyes had been pasted shut and had missed that.

But knowing his niece…

He gave an inner groan, his mind going back to the camera dangling on a cord around her neck.

Nothing he could do about that at the moment except take her inside and hope she forgot all about it by tomorrow morning.

The first thing he heard when he opened the door was a loud belch from somewhere inside.

Oh, hell. Not now.

He turned to Darcie. "Do you mind waiting here for a minute? I'll be right out."

Proving his point about his niece feigning sleep, her eyes popped open. "Oh, no. She has to come in. I want to take her back to see my room." She held up her camera. "We can look at the pictures I took on my computer."

"Luke? Is that you?" His brother's voice came from the living room, keeping him from commenting on Cora's suggestion. "I've been wondering when you were going to get home."

Felix *sounded* sober. Whether he was or not was another matter. "Yes, it's us."

Stepping in front of Darcie so he could enter first had nothing to do with being rude and everything to do with scoping out the situation. Cora was used to it—in fact, his niece had turned into a mother figure for her broken parent. But it was getting to the point where Lucas was going to have to intervene and take drastic action.

Again.

He set Cora on her feet but held her hand as they made their way to the living room, Darcie just behind him. There his brother sat in a recliner, staring at the television. Lucas glanced at the floor beside the chair. There was no sign of beer...or any other alcoholic beverage, for that matter. Could he have heard them come home and got rid of it? That burp had sounded pretty damning.

"Hey, girlie, come over here and give Daddy a hug."

Cora rushed over to her father and threw herself into his arms. That's when Lucas noticed the picture. The one of Felix, Cora and Melody taken in this very living room shortly after their daughter's birth. It was on the end table next to Felix and not in its normal spot on the fireplace mantel.

And when his brother's eyes met his they were red-rimmed.

He was drunk…maybe not from alcohol but from the deep grief that he refused to let go of. He held onto it as tightly as he did his liquor.

Damn. Don't do this now, Felix.

Unaware of what was going on, Darcie shifted next to him. His brain hummed as he tried to figure out a way to get her out of there without her realizing something was very wrong. Cora slid from her father's arms and hurried back to Darcie with a smile. "Come see my room."

Darcie's gaze took in Felix and then Lucas, as he stood there, jaw tight, fingers itching to curl into fists at his sides. He forced them to stay still instead. "Sure," she said to the little girl. "Let's go."

The pair trailed off down the hallway, while Lucas stared at his brother. "Have you been drinking?"

"Only one." He reached behind his back and pulled out an empty beer bottle. At least, Lucas hoped it had been empty before he'd secreted it behind him. "Something happened to the rest of them."

Lucas thought he'd dumped all the bottles. Evidently not. "Did you hide this one?"

"Yep." His brother waggled his head. "Good thing, too. Someone must have drunk all the rest of them. I think Chessa might have a drinking problem. Maybe we should fire her."

The childminder wasn't the one with a problem. It was his brother, in all his bitter glory.

"I dumped them. She didn't drink them."

"What?" His brother got to his feet, gripping the bottle in his fist. "You've got no right, Luke."

His voice went up ominously, causing Lucas to glance down the hall where Cora's door was wide open.

"Don't do this, Felix." He kept his own tone low and measured, hoping to lead by example.

"Don't *you* do this." Felix bit out the words. "You have no idea what it's like to lose someone important to you."

Yes, he did. He was watching it happen right before his eyes. Felix was a shell of the man he'd once been. A sad, drunken shell.

He decided to divert the subject if he could. He didn't want Cora or Darcie to hear his brother at his worst—or listen to the tears that would inevitably follow one of his tirades. "Are you taking your medication? You're not supposed to drink with it."

"I'm not."

Lucas wasn't sure if he meant he wasn't taking his medication or if he wasn't drinking. But since he was now shifting that bottle from one hand to the other, he would have to assume it was the latter. That he was off his antidepressants.

He took another quick look down the hallway then held his hand out for the beer bottle.

His brother surprisingly handed it over without an argument, probably because it was empty. He went over to the recycling bin and tossed it inside, hearing the clink as it landed on other bottles—hopefully the ones Lucas had emptied the other day.

When he went back he knew what he was going to say. "I love you, Felix, and I was hoping I'd never have to say this, but if you can't get your act together, Cora's going to have to come live with me for a while."

His brother shook his head, eyes wide. "You wouldn't take her from me. She's all I have left."

"I don't want to. But I can't leave her here to

watch you spiral back down, not when you've worked so hard over the last several months."

Felix sank into his chair. "I know. I need to pull it together, but…" He glanced at the picture of his wife.

With a sigh, Lucas took the picture and put it back in its spot on the mantelpiece just as Cora and Darcie came back into the room.

Darcie's face was pink and her glance went from him to Felix. Her hair was a riot of curls from their day at Max's and the sea air. It framed her face in a way that made his breath catch in his lungs. Lucas glanced at the group of pictures on the ledge over the fireplace.

Was this how his brother had started down that dark road? An initial attraction that had turned into an obsession that refused to let go, even after Melody's death?

Hell if he knew, but if that's the way it worked, he didn't even want to stop and glance at that road.

Hadn't he already? With both those kisses?

His jaw tightened and he glared at his brother. "Are you going to be okay tonight?"

"Yeah." Except Felix wouldn't quite meet his eyes. "Cora and I are going to be just fine. I've got big plans for us. Pizza and a movie. That one with all the singing and ice and snowmen."

His niece squealed. "I love that movie. You have to sing with me this time, Dad!"

"Yep, we're going to sing." He threw Lucas a defiant glare that dared him to argue with him.

He wouldn't, and his brother knew it. Not right now. But he would soon if Felix couldn't get back on track.

And if he had to take Cora away? What then for Felix?

That was one thing he didn't even want to think about. All he knew was that there came a time when the needs of his niece had to take precedence. And that time was drawing closer every day.

Darcie hadn't slept well. She wasn't sure if it was from looking at those pictures of her and Lucas frolicking in the pool or from the memories of him helping her take her restraints off.

That had to be it, because she certainly hadn't had a lot of restraint when it came to the man. And she needed some. Desperately. At least Cora hadn't captured that kiss they'd shared in the water.

She breathed a prayer of thanks.

Dressing quickly, she scowled at the dark circles beneath her eyes that told a tale of a long, hard night. There'd been those pictures, yes. But there'd also been something about Lucas's brother. He'd seemed just a little "off."

Not that she could pinpoint what made her think that. Cora had seemed happy enough when she'd interacted with him.

Maybe it was her coworker's behavior that had set her on edge and not Felix's.

Lucas had been tight-lipped the whole time he'd talked to his brother, and when she'd been in Cora's room, staring at those damning images, she'd thought she'd heard one of them raise his voice. She wasn't sure who it had been, though.

And it completely obliterated her view of Lucas as a self-indulgent playboy. His face had been deadly serious as he'd faced off with his brother. Were there hard feelings between the pair?

If so, he'd said nothing about it on the way back to her flat. And when she'd invited him up, he'd refused, saying he had an early morning. Well, so did she.

Another thing that had skewed her image of him. What man in his right mind would give up an opportunity to get into a woman's flat and into her pants?

Certainly not the Lucas she thought she knew.

Then again, she'd thought Cora was a full-grown woman back then. She didn't remember hearing Lucas talk about any other women over the months she'd known him. If anything, it was the other way around. Women talked about him. Wore false eyelashes for him. Threw themselves at him.

He hadn't taken the bait once that she knew of.

Maybe he's just not interested in you, dummy. He could have an unspoken rule about dating co-workers.

And kissing them? Did he have a rule against that too?

Not that she could tell. And she knew of at least a couple of the female species who would kill to have been in her shoes on either of those occasions.

Dwelling on this would get her nowhere. She tossed down the last of her tea with a sigh and went to finish dressing. At this rate, it was going to be one very long, depressing day.

Darcie made it to the maternity ward and signed in with just minutes to spare. Her eyes automatically tracked to the sign-in sheet, looking for Lucas's name. The space was blank. Strange. He wasn't here yet.

After all that blubbering about having an early day today? Irritation marched into her belly and kicked at its sides a couple of times. Maybe she'd been wrong after all. Maybe he did take the bait from time to time…just not when she was the one dangling it.

Fine. She wasn't going to wait around for him to check in.

Even as she thought it, she stood there and brooded some more, while the clock crept to three minutes past the hour, and the second hand began its downward arc, reminding her of Lucas's bungee jump yesterday. And, like yesterday, he was headed straight for the bottom… of her respect.

He was officially late. Again.

What was with the man? He never seemed irresponsible when you talked to him. But his actions? Another story.

Even as she thought it, Lucas came skidding around the corner, hair in glorious disarray, face sporting a dark layer of stubble. He took one glance at her and then took the pen and signed in. Five minutes late. Not enough to throw a fit about but he'd obviously not been home.

"Where were you?"

He flicked a glance her way then one brow went up in that familiar nonchalant manner that made her molars grind. "Keeping tabs on me, are you?"

She wanted to hurl at him, "You're late, and I want an explanation!" She wanted something other than his normal flippant response—the one that went along with the MMU's view of him: a charming playboy who took nothing seriously.

He'd diagnosed Margie Terrington, though, when she hadn't.

Because everyone in Victoria knew what red-back bite symptoms were.

Except her.

"No, of course not. I just…" For some reason she couldn't get the words out of her mouth, not while tears hovered around the periphery of her heart.

She would not beg him for an explanation. Or

ask him to reassure her that he wasn't this rumpled couldn't-care-less man who stood before her, as delicious as he looked.

He stepped closer. "I know I'm late. And I'm going to be later still once I go back and shower. But I'll make it quick." His jaw tightened. "All I can do, Darcie, is say I'm sorry."

Still not an answer. But at least all that glib cheekiness was gone.

She glanced at the patient board. "It's still quiet. I'll let Isla know you're here and that she can go home."

"Thanks." Warm fingers slid across her cheek and his glance dipped to her mouth before coming back up to her face.

Heat flashed up her spine. He wouldn't. Not here at work.

Before she could pull back—or remain locked in place, which was what her body wanted her to do—he withdrew his hand and took a step back.

"It would help me a lot if you didn't go all pink

every time you saw me—peace treaty or not, a man's only got so much willpower."

"I don't go pink!" Even as she said it, heat flamed up her neck and pooled in her cheeks, proving her a liar. It also broke the bubble of anger that had gathered around her.

Lucas laughed and tapped her nose. "Like I said…" He let the sentence trail away and then headed for the locker area, dragging both hands through his hair and whistling as he went.

Whistling!

Passing him in the hallway, Isla turned to glance at his retreating back before her eyes came to meet hers. Warmth again flooded her face as her friend drew near. "Well, I see he got here." She looked closer. "Why are you so red?"

"I—I…" What could she say, except deny it again?

"Oh, God. You two aren't…" Isla lowered her voice "…doing it, are you? I know I suggested he take you to the beach, but—"

Darcie reared back. "Of course not," she said in a loud whisper.

"Then why does the man look like he just rolled out of someone's bed? And why are we whispering? There's no one around."

Darcie cleared her throat and walked to the nurses' station. "We're whispering because I don't want any ugly rumors floating around about my personal life."

"Personal life?" Isla rubbed her belly. "You actually have one?"

The words might have stung had they not come from her friend. But Isla was right. "No. Can you blame me?"

Tessa came from a room with a chart in hand. She'd evidently overheard the last part of Darcie's declaration because she said, "You need to get out there and live it up a bit. Melbourne has some awesome nightclubs. Maybe we could make it a group outing."

"I don't know…"

Isla took up the cry. "Yes! You have to go at least once. I can't believe I didn't take you."

"You were kind of busy, remember?" An understatement if there ever was one.

Her friend laughed, hand still on her burgeoning stomach. "Maybe just a little. But, seriously, you can't leave Australia without seeing at least a little of the nightlife."

The three of them were still joking about it when Lucas appeared less than ten minutes later. Wow, the man was fast, she'd give him that. His hair was damp from his shower and he'd changed into fresh clothes.

"What are we talking about, ladies?"

"Oh…nothing." Even as she said it the slow flush rose in her face like clockwork. One side of his mouth lifted but, thank God, he said nothing about it this time.

Isla nudged her. "Darcie hasn't been to any of the nightspots. None. Zip. Can you believe it?"

"It seems there's quite a lot she hasn't experienced yet."

Lucas said it with a totally straight face, but she glanced sharply at him.

Tessa cocked her head, drumming her short fingernails on the counter. "Maybe I can get a group together to go to the Night Owl tonight. They have brilliant music and dancing. How does that sound, Darcie?"

"Well, I..." She didn't dance if she could help it. Another thing that had worn thin with Robert, who had loved it.

"If Darcie's going to make a checklist of things to do while in Australia, that should definitely go on it."

Great, just what she needed, to have him remind her of his challenge—that she pick things that were outside her comfort zone. Clubbing was definitely one of those. Not that any of them had suggested making the rounds and getting drunk.

She tried one last time. "I have to work tomorrow."

Lucas parried with, "We'll watch our step and make sure you're not arrested."

"Arrested!"

Isla put a hand on her arm. "He's kidding. You should go, Darcie. Especially since Lucas seems to be offering his services as a bouncer. You know, in case a thousand guys start hitting on you. I, unfortunately, am not allowed to have any fun for another month or so, even if Alessi would agree to let me go."

Darcie snuck a glance at Lucas, who didn't look at all put out with the idea of tagging along.

The nurse picked up a chart with a grin. "I have to go back to work now, unlike some of you. I'll ask around and whoever wants to come can meet up at the entrance of the hospital at eight, okay? Wear something sparkly."

And with that, Tessa and Lucas both walked away without giving her a chance to refuse. And the hunky midwife had left without actually confirming that he would be there—protecting her from unwanted advances.

Unfortunately, if he did come, Darcie had no idea who was going to save her from him—or from herself.

CHAPTER SIX

SHE'D WORN SOMETHING SPARKLY. And green. And clingy as hell.

That dress was probably banned in ten countries. There was nothing vulgar about it, but the neckline scooped far enough down that a hint of creamy curves peeked over the top of it. And it was snug around her hips and the sweet curve of her backside, exposing an endless length of bare leg. He'd been trying not to stare as the group of them had taken off from the hospital and headed toward the railway station. But, holy hell, it was hard.

"Did you go shopping?" Because he just couldn't see Darcie pulling something like this out of her wardrobe. Not that he was complaining. No, he was salivating. And thinking about all the men at that club who were going to see her in this dress was doing a number on his gut.

"No. Isla loaned it to me. I didn't bring anything suitable for a night on the town."

Suitable. That was one word for it. What it was suitable for was the question. Because in his mind he could see himself peeling the thing down her shoulders and right past all those sexy curves. They might just get arrested after all.

Why had he agreed to come again?

Oh, yes. To ward off any unwanted advances. If that was the case, he was going to have his hands full. Because he might end up having to fight off his own advances if he couldn't get his damned libido under control. Right now it was raging and growling and doing all it could to edge closer to this woman.

Thank God, the train ride was a short one. And there were seats this time, instead of having to stand and have her bump against him repeatedly. Within another few minutes they arrived at the

Night Owl, a club frequented by young professionals looking to let their hair down.

The second the doors opened the music hit him between the eyes. Loud, with a driving beat, blast after blast of sound pumped out into the night air. Despite his cocky words earlier in the day, Lucas had not gone to a club since his early days at medical school. Life had been too hectic, and after Melody had died he just hadn't had much else on his mind except his brother and Cora.

Ten people in all had come with them. The rest of the group went in, but when Darcie started to pass through the door she backed up as if changing her mind, only to crash into his chest. Her backside nestled against him for a split second before she jerked away again.

His internal systems immediately went haywire.

That decided it. He wanted to be here. With her. For whatever reason.

Maybe it was just to escape the highs and lows that had become a normal part of life these last years. He'd enjoyed the bungee-jumping trip far too much. He was ready to repeat the energetic day. But in all-adult company this time. The club would do that and more.

Strangely, the noise would insulate them, keep their words from being overheard by those around them.

When she again hesitated he leaned down. "It's okay, Darce. I'm right here with you."

There was that short version of her name again, sliding right past his lips like it belonged there. He didn't know why that kept happening, but it did the trick. She stepped through the door. And as if he'd fallen down the rabbit hole in that old children's book, the inside of the club morphed into something from another place and time.

Darkness bathed the occupants, except for brief snatches of light that flooded his pupils. The extremes made it hard to focus on anything for more than a second at a time so bodies became puppets, moving in jolts and jerks as if controlled by outside forces. The sensation was surreal. Anything that happened in the club to-night would take on a dreamlike quality: had it happened, or hadn't it? Maybe that was for the best.

Tessa came back and grabbed Darcie by the arm, dragging her away and making a drinking motion with her hand, since it was probably impossible for her to yell above the noise.

When had it become noise? At one time in his life he would have been yelling for the DJ to turn the sound up. Not any more. He squinted, trying to see where the group from the hospital had gone. When he trained his eyes to capture the second-long flashes emitted by the strobe he could just make out the dim overhead lights of the bar at the far side of the room. At least those weren't blinking on and off.

A few minutes later he was there, squeezed between Darcie and some guy on her left—who shot him a look that could only be described as a glare. The man picked up his drink and moved on to another woman a few seats away. Tessa laughed and saluted him with her drink, while the glass in front of Darcie contained something that looked fruity and cold, with plenty of crushed ice—and probably a shot of something strong. The bartender came over with a quizzical lift of his brows.

"Just a lemonade," he yelled above the music.

Darcie threw him a wide-eyed glance. "I thought we were supposed to be living dangerously."

"I still have to get you home in one piece, so it's better for me to play it safe. At least for tonight." Lucas had had enough of Felix's drinking problems to last a lifetime. Except for that swig of beer he'd taken in his brother's kitchen, he hadn't touched the stuff in almost two years.

Some of their party had broken off into pairs and were already out on the dance floor—he squinted again—if that could be called dancing. The body parts moved, but they were disjointed…staccato. Although maybe that had to do with the lights blinking on and off.

Darcie put her straw to her mouth and took a sip of her drink then stirred the concoction while glancing around at the nightclub. The Night Owl was living up to its name, although it seemed a little early for the die-hard crowd. How much more packed could the place get?

"Are these kinds of things big in Australia?" she shouted.

This was ridiculous. They were both going to be hoarse by the time they got to work tomorrow if they kept this up. He drew her closer and leaned down to her ear. "I'm not a big nightclub person."

She tilted back to look at him then moved back in. "You bungee jump, but you don't go out drinking with the guys?"

Her warm breath washed across his ear, carrying the scent of her drink. Strawberries. Or mangoes. Okay, so maybe this wasn't going to be the disaster he was imagining because he liked having her close like this.

The guy from the seat next to him had evidently

struck out with woman number two, because he was back. Bodily inserting himself between the two of them and turning his back to Lucas.

"Dance?"

He couldn't blame the guy. Darcie was beautiful. But if anyone was going to dance with her, it was going to be him.

Standing, he poked the intruder in the shoulder to get his attention. The man—a body-builder type with bulges and lumps that bordered on unnatural—didn't budge. So Lucas moved out and around until he was facing the competition.

Darcie was already shaking her head to the offer. Instead of taking the hint, the jerk held out his hand.

Lucas stared him straight in the eye. "She's with me, mate. So try somewhere else." Taking her hand, he said, "Come on, gorgeous. Bring your drink."

She grabbed her glass and went along with him, throwing the other man an apologetic look. What the hell? Had she wanted to dance with him?

This time it was Lucas who hesitated. He stopped and glanced down at her.

"Here, try some," she said, holding her beverage up to him. "It's really good."

As much as he did not want to try some girly-girl drink, he noted the creep from the bar was still glowering their way. Probably hoping to corner her alone. To send another message, he took the glass from her and sipped from the straw…and made a face. He couldn't help it. That wasn't a drink. That was some kind of smoothie or something. But the act of putting his mouth where her lips had been—where they had applied suction and…

He took another sip. A bigger one this time and let it wash down his throat. Not so bad the second time around.

Handing it back to her, he towed her further out onto the floor, where dark forms kicked and flapped and buckled, only to come up for more. It reminded him more of a fight scene from a movie than actual dancing.

Flashes of green from her eyes met his. "I'm not much of a dancer."

There was something about the way she said it. As if she expected him to be upset. Hardly.

She couldn't be any worse than what was going on around him. "Let's pretend the music is slow and not worry about what everyone else is doing." He'd had to swoop in again to be heard. "Can you dance with your glass in your hand?"

"No. Help me finish it." She took another drink, the contents of the large goblet dropping a quarter of an inch, then held it out to him again.

He was going to pay for this later, when the memories came back to haunt him in his sleep. But he drank anyway. Relished the slight taste of her on the straw.

When the glass was empty he motioned for her to wait and then deposited it on the nearest table, ignoring the surprised looks from its occupants. Then he strode back to Darcie and took her right hand in his, his other arm settling across her hips and pulling her close. When his attention swept the bar for the man who'd hit on her, he didn't see him. Good. Because tonight there would be no cutting in.

Darcie was all his. At least for a few hours.

If Cora didn't call.

Closing his eyes and settling her against him, he allowed his senses to absorb the feel of her curves, the scent of her hair and the way it slid like fine silk beneath his chin.

He tuned out the music…and tuned in Darcie instead. Only then did he allow his feet to sway, taking quarter-inch steps and allowing his inner rhythm to take over. Her arm crept up, her hand splaying across the skin on the back of his neck, fingers pushing into the hair at his nape.

Decadent.

Isla was right. There were some things that just shouldn't be missed. And dancing with Darcie was one of them.

She shifted against him with a sigh. "This is much better than what they're doing."

"Who?" His eyes cracked open, letting the chaotic scene back into his head.

"Everyone. I don't normally like to dance. But this feels okay."

"Yes, it does."

The song ended and the room paused for three or four seconds, while Lucas cursed silently. Then, as if the universe had read his mind, another song came on. This was slow and soothing and not quite as loud. The atmosphere shifted. The strobe went off in favor of dim, steady lighting.

Arms twined together and single dancers edged off the floor to let the couples have a turn.

"Is this better?" he murmured into her ear.

"Mmm, yes."

Lucas's hand tightened on her back, thumb skimming up her spine and drawing his palm along with it until it was between her shoulder blades, before gliding back down to her waist.

Hell, this was nice. Maybe a little too nice.

Darcie must have sensed it too because the fingertips that were against the lower part of his scalp brushed back and forth, sending a frisson of raw sensation arrowing down to his groin.

He willed away the rush of need that followed, trying to think about anything else but the pulsing that was beginning to make itself known in not-so-subtle ways.

Football. Kayaking. Hiking.

He dragged various activities through his head and forced his brain to come up with five important items about each one, before moving on to the next. Anything to keep from having to step back a pace or two in order to hide her effect on him.

Because he didn't want to go. Not until this song was over and done. And maybe not even then.

There. Things were subsiding. Slowly. But as long as she didn't…

Her fingertips dragged downward, emerging from his hair and sliding sideways across the bare skin of his neck.

"Darce, are you trying to make me crazy?" Because if he didn't say something, she was going to end up with one hell of a surprise.

Her cheek moved away from his chest and she glanced up at him. "I wasn't trying to. Why, am I succeeding?"

Something about the way she'd said that. As if surprised. Or curious. Or a whole lot of things. None of them good because it just stirred him to say more stupid things. They'd all agreed to leave separately, so they could each decide when they'd had enough. But no way was he letting Darcie leave there on her own.

"Yes." He let that one word speak for him, because it was true.

"So I can cross this off my list, right?"

"Driving me crazy?"

"No." She gave a soft laugh. "I was talking about coming to a nightclub."

His brows went up, and he realized without that godawful strobe light he could finally see her without the additional shock on his senses.

Being this close to her was as heady as laying her down on the sand at the beach had been. "I thought you might be angling to finally cross something else off your list."

Her tongue came out, moistening that full lower lip. "What's that?"

She was going to make him say it, wasn't she? "Kissing an Aussie."

"But I thought you said that had to be behind closed doors in order to count." The breathiness of her response made him smile.

"It does. But that can be arranged."

Her fingers at the back of his neck tightened, and her eyes closed for a second.

Was she going to turn him down? His body started to groan and swear at him for screwing this up. Maybe he should limit it to just the kiss. But, hell, he didn't want just a kiss. He wanted to carry her down some dark hallway and toss her on a bed…expose every luscious inch of her. And *then* kiss her.

When her eyelids parted again she gave a nod.

"Then yes. But only if it's a wild and outrageous kiss."

He couldn't resist. He leaned down and nipped the jawline next to her ear. "Trust me. I can make that happen."

The song ended, and Lucas realized he and Darcie were no longer dancing. In fact, they were just standing there in each other's arms, staring at each other.

"Let's go back to Isla's flat."

"What?" He pulled back, thinking he'd surely misunderstood. He wanted to be alone with her, not visit Isla and Alessandro.

She laughed, unwinding her arm from around his neck and grabbing his hand as she made her way off the dance floor. "I mean the Delamere flat, where I'm staying. Alone."

That was more like it. Besides, that end of town was closer than his own place. And his barely furnished flat left little to be desired as far as what she was probably used to. "That sounds like a plan. Lead on."

* * *

Darcie was somehow able to find her keys in the tiny glittery purse that she'd slung over her shoulder as they'd left the Night Owl and arrived at the large opulent building Charles Delamere owned. She punched the code into the box by the front door and heard the click as it unlocked. She'd seen it so many times the place didn't even register any more, but with Lucas standing there behind her she suddenly felt self-conscious as they made their way across the marble foyer.

"You've been here before, right?" She didn't want him to get the idea that she was rich or anything. But she'd never thought anything less of Isla for living here, so why would she think Lucas was any different?

Maybe because it mattered what he thought, and she wasn't quite sure why.

"I have. Isla liked to entertain, so I've been here several times."

Entertain. As in a group? Or just Lucas? "Oh, um…"

"We were never involved," he murmured, as if sensing her thoughts.

"Oh, I didn't think—"

"Didn't you? You thought I might be involved with a whole horde of females at one time."

She had. And when had she moved so far away from that initial opinion she'd held of him? Maybe when she'd met Cora and seen how much he cared about his niece. And maybe—when she put all those phone calls into context—they'd become sweet. Whatever it was, she no longer believed many of the things she'd once thought.

"People change," she murmured.

His hand tightened on hers for a second and his footsteps faltered.

Had she said something wrong?

"Yes, they do."

They stopped in front of the lift and Darcie punched the button to call it. Lucas leaned a shoulder against the wall next to her and studied her face, a slight frown between his brows. Right on cue, heat surged into her cheeks.

His mood seemed to clear and he smiled. "I don't think I've ever seen a woman blush as much as you do."

"I can't help it. It's just the way I'm made."

His eyes skimmed down the rest of her, pausing at the neckline of Isla's slinky dress. "I'm kind of partial to the way you're made."

Her face grew even hotter and he chuckled. Then the lift arrived, saving her from having to respond to his comment.

They both got on, and Darcie nodded at the camera tucked into the corner of the lift, hoping he'd understand her meaning.

He did, because he leaned down, his warm breath washing over her cheek. "Don't worry, gorgeous. I don't want an audience this time. Although later…"

When her eyes widened, his hand went to her lower back, fingertips skimming up her spine until he reached her nape. One finger made tiny circles there beneath the curtain of her hair. Pure need spiraled through her as he added a second finger, the pair trailing down and around the back of her dress, which was scooped like the front of it was. To the camera, it would appear as if they were both just standing quietly, but inside her chest her heart was jumping and things were heating up.

A fine layer of perspiration broke out on her upper lip as she struggled not to close her eyes or utter the soft sounds that were bubbling up in her throat. Was there a microphone connected to that camera?

Up, up they went, racing toward the penthouse while Darcie's legs turned to jelly, and the need to touch him back began growing in her chest. In her belly. In her hands.

She curled her fingers into her palms to keep them from reaching for him.

"Do you like that?" he whispered.

Was he joking? Couldn't he tell? She glanced at their reflection in the mirror across from them and noted her nipples were puckered, showing even through the fabric of her strapless bra and her dress, although both were thin.

Ping.

The lift slowed, and Lucas stopped stroking her neck, his warm hand wrapping around her nape instead. When the doors opened, she practically fell out onto the dark glossy floor of the entrance to the flat. Hands shaking, she tried to hit the lock with her key and missed the first time, only to have Lucas's fingers cover hers and guide them to the keyhole, unlocking and opening the door in one smooth movement.

They went inside. "D-do you want a tour?"

"Mmm…yes, but not of the flat." He took the keys from her hand and the purse from her shoulder and put them both on the slate surface of the entry table.

Her teeth dug into her lower lip as Lucas came back and put his hands on her shoulders, thumbs edging just beneath the fabric covering them. This was a man who bungee-jumped and practically made love to her on an open beach. Who teased and tormented her senses on the dance floor and again in the lift. He didn't want a feeble tour or a half-hearted response from whatever woman he was with.

Robert's face as Tabitha had thrown herself into his arms was branded in her mind. That was what her ex-fiancé had wanted. Not a mild-mannered woman who was far too "safe."

Was Lucas going to find her wanting as well? Would he regret having put all this effort into getting her into bed?

That brought up another question. Was that why he'd done everything he had…the trip to the beach, the list, the nightclub? To sleep with her? Her insecurities grew.

She had no illusions that this was anything but a one-night stand. She'd made it clear that she didn't want anything more than that either. But maybe she should make it clear that she probably wasn't as wildly experienced as some of the women he'd been with.

"I—I'm not…" She licked her lips as Lucas

went still. "I'm probably not very good at…" Her voice died away a second time, so she had to use her hand to made swirly motions in the air and hope he got the gist of her meaning.

He tightened his grip on her shoulders slightly. "Please, tell me you're not a virgin."

"No!" The denial came out as a squeak, so she cleared her throat. "My fiancé just found me a bit…dull in that respect."

Lucas didn't move for several seconds, but a muscle pulsing in his cheek made her squirm. Was he wondering how to get out of the flat without hurting her feelings?

"You don't have to stay if you don't want to." There. She'd given him a way to escape.

He shook his head. "I'm not planning on going anywhere, unless you decide to throw me out." He then gave a smile that could only be described as rueful. "My experience with you has been anything but dull."

She remembered his curse when he'd seen her name on that rotation list. Actually, she had been more outspoken with him than she was with most people. But only because he'd irritated her with his attitude and his tardiness. Okay, so maybe she wasn't dull at work. But here? "I'm not very adventurous."

He leaned down and gave her a slow kiss. One that started off soft and easy and gradually built…his hand sliding into her hair and gathering the strands in his fist. When he pulled back again she was breathless and right back to where she'd been in the lift—melting with desire and wanting nothing more than for him to drag her down those three steps to the living area and take her right there on the couch.

"Then you won't mind if I'm adventurous enough for both of us."

The pressure of being someone she wasn't lifted. She could do that. She could let Lucas call the shots and introduce her to things she'd never tried before—just like he had standing on that high tower, and again after she'd landed in the pool.

This man lit her senses up like no one ever had. "No. I won't mind."

"Well, then." He began bunching her dress in his fists, gathering more and more material in them until the hemline was at the very tops of her thighs. "We won't need this." Up and over her head went the dress, which had no zipper, the stretchy material allowing him to strip it off her body with ease. He turned and carried the garment across the space, going lightly down the steps and placing it over one of the leather chairs in the living room.

When she started to follow him, he held up his hand to signal her to wait. He slowly made his way back up, his eyes on her the whole time. "You're beautiful, Darce. I don't know what your ex told you, but 'dull' is not a word I would ever use to describe you."

He reached for her hands as a warm flush crept up her body. It only increased when he carried her hands behind her back and moved in to kiss her again. This one slow and lingering, his lips brushing across hers, the friction driving her crazy. "Where's your bedroom, sweetheart?"

"Down the hall. First door to the right."

"Down the hall we go, then." Before she could move he released her hands and swept her into his arms as if she weighed nothing.

He arrived at her room and edged her through the door, stopping for a second as if to take in the space. Although she was sleeping in Isabel's old room, she'd boxed up the other woman's mementos and substituted a few things she'd brought with her. But other than that the space was devoid of a lot of personal items other than the bed and dresser. There were built-ins that were still almost empty.

Walking over to the queen-size bed that had her wondering if it would hold Lucas's frame, he glanced down at her, eyes unreadable. "You never planned on sticking around, did you?"

She was surprised by the question. Everyone at the hospital knew she was only here for a year. After that she'd be leaving. Had he expected her to fill the room with stuff, only to have to get rid of it all a few short months later? And that's what it was looking like at this point: a few short months. Her time in Australia had flown by. Much quicker than she'd thought it would. But it had done what she'd intended it to do—erased the pain of Robert and Tabitha's betrayal. "You knew I was only here for a year."

His muscles relaxed, as if she'd given the correct response. Except she didn't know what the real question was. That he didn't want her to stick around, because of the conflict that had flared between them periodically? Or that he was making sure she wasn't going to place any more importance on tonight than he planned to? He didn't have to worry on that account. She'd already bought her return ticket months ago, right after their first big blow-up.

She blinked up at him. "Are you sure you want to stay?"

"You keep asking me that as if you hope I'll

change my mind." He dropped her on the bed and then followed her down. "I won't."

She wound her arms around his neck. "Well, okay, then. As long as we're both clear on what happens on the other side, we should be good."

"Let's worry about right now. And then we can deal with the other stuff tomorrow." With that, his mouth came down, blotting out everything except for the fact that this was exactly where Darcie wanted to be. In this man's arms.

CHAPTER SEVEN

HE WAS GOING to make this a night she would remember.

Not because he was that good but because her words had picked at a sore spot within him. No, he didn't want any permanent relationships, but he was stung by how easy she seemed to think it would be to walk away from him. An idiotic response, considering his own attitude, but he'd never been a rational man when it came to Darcie.

Her bra had no straps to peel down so he settled for following the course of an imaginary strap with his fingers, making sure his short nails kept light contact with her skin as they made their way across her shoulders.

Her reaction was to arch a few centimeters off the silk duvet cover. His flesh reacted in kind.

Arching up and away from his body, only to be stopped by the fabric of his dress trousers. That would soon be remedied. But not quite yet.

He continued down her arms, going past the crook of her elbows and only stopping when he reached her wrists, which he caught up in both of his hands. He carried them over her head and rested them there, catching sight of bright green eyes as they stared at his face. He wanted her hands out of the way for what he did next.

Her lips were parted and glossy from his kisses, so he leaned in for another quick taste, glorying in the way they clung to his and followed him up an inch or two as he moved away. He gave a pained laugh.

Dull? Hell, her ex was an idiot. This woman was responsive, giving, and sexy as they came. She hadn't put any limits on their time together. When he'd said he was going to be adventurous enough for both of them, her glance had heated instantly.

Which brought him back to his point. He

wanted to make this good. Wanted to leave her with no doubt that she was exciting and desirable. Not just to him but to plenty of other men. He'd caught Max's glances at her during the bungee jump. And the guy at the bar? Oh, he'd been interested all right. The thought made his blood pressure shoot up, just as it had at the Night Owl.

Hooking one of his legs between hers, he edged her thighs apart, keeping his foot just behind her ankle in case she was tempted to squeeze them shut again. She didn't even try. That in itself made Lucas's flesh surge, putting up some new demands. He was willing to oblige some of them…but others would have to wait.

He let his fingers slide over the sweet curves peeking just above her bra. Her skin was smooth and incredibly soft. He wanted more. Keeping his leg between hers, he reached beneath her body and searched for the clasp. Found it. Flicked it open.

He then dropped the garment over the side of the bed, and drank in the view before him.

Heavenly. In every way.

Her nipples were drawn up tight—pink and perfect. Darcie's eyes were open now. She made no move to cover herself with her hands, although her breathing ratcheted up a notch.

That was as far as he got before he could stand it no longer. He leaned down and tasted her, drawing one peak into his mouth and letting his tongue wander over it.

She moaned and arched higher, pushing herself into his touch.

Yes. This was what he needed. He applied more pressure, using her response as a gauge for how much friction she wanted from him.

Hell if she didn't ask him to up the ante even more. When his teeth scraped over her, her hands came down on his head, but instead of pulling him away her fingers buried themselves in his hair and she pushed hard against him.

He came up panting, body raging, wanting to end it all right here, right now. Instead, he let his mouth cover hers, tongue plunging inside again and again, while she maintained her grip on his hair.

Pulling away in a rush, he ripped her undies down and found her hot and wet and ready. He kissed her once again, letting his index finger sink deep into her. Just like he was about to. He got off the bed.

"Do. Not. Move." He growled the words, stripping in record time, letting the sight of her flushed body drive him to action—to find the condom and rip into it, sheathing himself.

Then he was back with her, over her. Finding her. Sliding home to a place where pleasure and madness fought for supremacy.

He set up a slow, easy rhythm that was all for her, ignoring his own wants and needs.

"Lucas." His name was whispered. Shaky. A silent plea he couldn't ignore.

"I'm here, gorgeous." He edged out and then pushed deep.

Darcie responded with a long drawn-out moan,

lifting her hips, her hands going to his shoulders and holding on.

Kissing and licking the length of her neck, he allowed her tight heat to wash over him in a wave, careful to hang onto whatever control he still had. He wanted this to last.

And that surprised him.

He usually saw to his partner's pleasure first and then concentrated on his own. He had it down to a science almost. But here he was, breaking his own rules. She hadn't climaxed. And he didn't want her to. Not yet. He wanted to lose himself when she did—wanted to watch the exact second she came apart. He could only do that if he knew when…

He rolled over, carrying her with him until she was on top, straddling his hips. Her eyes jerked open, and she looked at him uncertainly.

"You set the pace, Darcie. Do what feels good to you."

While I watch.

She hesitated for a second then her instincts

seemed to take over. She braced her hands on his thighs, just behind her butt and lifted up and came back down as if seeing how it felt. Then her eyes fluttered shut, teeth digging into her bottom lip as she moved over him a second time. Then a third. Again and again, she lowered herself onto him and rose back up. His own personal angel, set on propelling them both toward paradise.

Until Lucas began to ache from holding back. It was time.

Pressing his palm against her lower belly, he allowed his thumb to find that sensitive place between her thighs. Her head went back, little whimpers coming from her throat and spilling into the air around him. Sexy sounds. Earthy and full of need.

Her movements grew jerky, hands tightening on his thighs.

"Yes, sweetheart, that's it," he gritted. "Let it all go."

With that, Darcie's whole body stiffened, her insides flaring for a split second before clamping down hard on his erection and exploding into a series of spasms that rocked his world, that made him grab her hips and pump wildly, washing her orgasm down with his own. He poured every emotion he had into the act, until there was nothing left.

And yet he was still full. Full of Darcie. Full of those luscious aftershocks that had him pulling her down hard onto him, eyes closed as he absorbed all of it and more.

When he looked up again her eyes were open. Looking at him. A trembling question in those bright green depths.

She had doubts?

He drew her down until she was lying across his chest, her face nestled against his neck. "You okay?"

"Mmm-hmm." A hesitation. "You?"

"Perfect. Absolutely perfect." He leaned down and kissed the top of her head. "And you're about to cross one thing off your list."

"The kiss?"

He should say yes. End it once and for all. It would be on a good note. One they could both smile about years from now. But he didn't want to. Not with his body already beginning to reset itself. So he said instead, "Not yet. I'll tell you when."

With that he rolled her back beneath him and pressed his mouth to hers.

Darcie had been walking around in a daze.

Beginning with the moment she'd woken up in an empty bed. For some reason, she'd thought Lucas would wake her to say goodbye if he decided to leave. He hadn't. But after the second lovemaking session she'd been exhausted. And replete. And something about going to sleep with his arm anchoring her close to his body had given her a sense of comfort she hadn't felt in a long time.

How long had he stayed once she'd drifted off? A few minutes? An hour?

The only thing that had made her smile—since

she'd been squirming with embarrassment over some of her actions—had been that Lucas had ticked the "kiss a non-triangular Aussie" box and drawn an arrow out to a smiley face. *A smiley face*. She'd never known a man to use one before.

And the fact that he'd rolled out of her bed and actually felt like smiling made a lump come to her throat. She'd assumed with Robert it had been her problem...that he'd been rejecting her. Maybe he'd been rejecting them as a couple. Because although Lucas had used the word "uptight" when he'd grumbled about that roster, he hadn't given any indication last night that he still found her that way.

Instead, he'd smiled.

She kept twisting that fact round and round in her head. It had to have meant he was as satisfied as she was, right?

Grabbing the clipboard for her next patient, she glanced at the name. Margie Terrington, their redback bite patient. She glanced at her mobile phone, wondering if she should call Lucas in to join her for the consultation, but she was leery. She hadn't actually spoken to him yet today. Why ruin her mood before she had to?

She pushed through the door, only to stop short. Lucas was already in the room. But, then, why was the chart…?

He glanced at her with an undecipherable expression. "I thought you might eventually make it to work today."

Eventually make it? She'd been twenty minutes early, just like most days. Which meant he'd been…

Even earlier.

The very corners of his mouth went up, making her heart lift along with them, but she was careful not to let on to her patient that Lucas was teasing her. "I did indeed." She greeted Margie and flipped through her chart, asking a few questions.

Lucas sat and listened to the back and forth for a minute or two before asking his own question. "Any problems from the antivenin?"

"None." The expectant mum rubbed her belly. "I can't thank you both enough for figuring out what was wrong."

"Thank Lucas, he was the one who realized you'd been bitten."

The young woman shuddered. "My husband tore the rest of the house apart to make sure there weren't any more of them."

They finished checking her over, letting her listen to the baby's heartbeat to reassure her that all was indeed well after the scare the previous week. "Did your mum come to Australia? With your husband working, I know it'll be a great help to have her here. We could all use a little support." As Darcie well knew from her parents' support after what Robert had done.

They'd been thrilled that she'd been able to go to Australia to get away from everything that had happened. She'd barely prevented her dad from punching her ex-fiancé right in the nose. But she'd grabbed his arm at the last moment. Everyone had parted semi-amicably. And the only heart that had been broken that day had been hers. She'd been left in the wedding chapel all alone after everyone had left—her mum seeing to all the last-minute explanations and canceling the venue for the honeymoon.

"Yes, she arrived just a few days ago," Margie said. "She already loves it here. And, yes, we could all use the support of family. After our other…loss…I wondered if I would ever be happy again. I thought I'd never get over it."

Lucas stood with a suddenness that made both women look at him. He glanced at Darcie and then away, muttering that he needed to check on another patient.

She frowned.

That look wasn't anything that resembled a smiley face. And she had no idea who that "other patient" could be because there wasn't anyone listed on the schedule board for another hour. There were a couple of patients in rooms, and she'd noticed one poor woman was curled on her side, sucking down nitrous oxide with a rather desperate air, but they all had other midwives attending them. After saying goodbye to Margie, she went into the hallway and glanced down the corridor, but there was no sign of him. Darcie had hoped to talk to him about how they were going to treat last night.

Already one of the other nurses had cornered her and asked why she'd left the nightclub so early. She'd feigned a headache and said she'd caught the train back to her flat. Not a total lie. But she certainly wasn't going to tell anyone she'd dragged Lucas home with her. She couldn't even bring herself to admit all they'd done together, much less admit it to anyone else. It would be much better if they had some kind of joint cover story to hand out to anyone who asked. Present a united front, as it were.

Even if they weren't united.

Oh, well. Stepping outside the hospital to get a breath of fresh air, she heard her name being called. Not by Lucas but by a child. Darcie swung round in time to see Cora and her dad coming toward them on the footpath. Cora broke into a run and gave her a fierce hug as soon as she reached her, Felix trailing along behind. When he finally caught up he looked a bit shamefaced and maybe even a little shaken up. "Do you know where my brother is?"

"I don't. We just finished up with a patient, though, so he's here somewhere." Darcie didn't want to admit that she had no idea where he'd gone or why. Her stomach was beginning to do a slow dive to the bottom of her abdominal cavity, though.

"I can stay here with Darcie, Dad. She won't mind, will you?"

Felix scratched the back of his neck. "I don't know, Cora. I think we should just go home."

"But you can't! You promised me, and you promised Uncle Luke." Cora's voice came across shrill and upset.

If anything, her father looked even more unsure. "I know, but Chessa is sick and I'm not leaving you home alone."

Darcie didn't have any idea what was going on, but whatever it was sounded important, judging from Cora's overly bright eyes. Tears? Looking to defuse the situation, she said, "Why don't I try to reach his mobile and see where he is?"

But when she tried to do that, the phone went right to voicemail. Strange. Unless he had it off so he wouldn't have to talk to her. His behavior in Margie's room had set her alarm bells ringing earlier. And now this. Her stomach dropped even further. She settled for leaving a message. "Hello, Lucas, it's Darcie." Why she felt compelled to explain who she was when he would know from the caller ID was beyond her. She went on, "Felix and Cora are here at the south entrance. Would you mind stopping round if you get this within the next few minutes?"

She pressed the disconnect button, only to have Cora tell her, "We tried to ring him too, but he didn't answer."

That didn't sound like Lucas. He doted on his niece. "I could keep her here with me for a while.

I have an office where she could hang out until Lucas turns up."

A look of profound gratitude went through Felix's eyes. "Are you sure it's no trouble? I have an appointment and our childminder is ill."

"It's fine. Leave it to me." She took Cora by the hand. "We'll get on famously until then."

Felix looked uncertain for all of five seconds then he nodded. "Okay, I appreciate it."

"Bye, Daddy," Cora said. "Maybe Uncle Luke can drive me home and get me an ice lolly on the way."

Darcie's heart twisted. So much for hoping he might want to come home with her. Again.

What? Are you insane?

Evidently, because her mind had, in fact, already traveled down that path and was trying to figure out a way to make it come true.

Giving Felix her mobile number and waving him off with what she hoped was a cheerful toss of her head, she made her way back inside the hospital, Cora following close behind.

Once in her office, the little girl found a pull-apart model of a baby in a pregnant belly that Darcie kept to show her patients. She'd forgotten it was on her desk when she'd offered to bring Cora here. "I'm not sure your dad would want you looking at that."

"Oh, I know all about how babies are born. Uncle Luke's a midwife. I have to know."

Darcie couldn't stop the smile. "You do, do you? And why is that?"

"Because I'm going to be a midwife too. Did you know that Uncle Luke helped my mum have me? She couldn't make it to a hospital."

No, she hadn't known, because Lucas hadn't talked about anything personal, she realized. In fact, he knew some pretty intimate stuff about her, while she knew almost nothing about him. Like whether or not his parents were still alive. Or why he'd gone into midwifery in the first place.

Because it was none of her business.

Careful not to pump the girl for information,

she settled for a noncommittal response that she hoped would end the conversation.

It didn't. "Mummy died of cancer."

That she *did* know. "I'm sorry, Cora."

"I don't remember much about her. But I do remember she always smelled nice…like chocolate biscuits."

Darcie swallowed hard, forcing down the growing lump in her throat. What would it be like to lose your mother at such a tender age? Her own mum was still her very best friend and confidante. She decided to change the subject once and for all, since neither Felix nor Lucas would appreciate knowing her and Cora's chat had revealed old heartaches. "Speaking of biscuits, Cora, would you like to go down to the café and see if they have something good to eat? I'll just let the nurses know where I'll be."

"Yay!" Cora grabbed her hand and tugged her toward the door. "Does the coffee shop have espresso, do you think?"

She gave the little girl a sharp glance, not sure

if she was joking or not. "How about we both stick with hot chocolate?"

"Even better. Daddy sometimes forgets to buy the chocolate powder."

"Then hot chocolate we shall have."

Fifteen minutes later they were in the cafeteria at a table, with Cora imitating the way Darcie drank her chocolate. It made Darcie smile. She could see why Lucas was so very fond of her. The girl was exuberant and full of life, despite the tragedy she'd suffered at such a young age. Then again, children were resilient, a characteristic she often wished was carried into adulthood.

The buzzer on her phone went off and when she looked at the screen her eyes widened. Lucas. He must have got her message. She answered, forcing herself to speak cheerfully, even though her heart was cranking out signals of panic. "Hi."

"May I ask where you are, and why my niece is with you? You're not in your office."

"I…uh…" Oh, God, it hadn't been her imagination in Margie's room. He *was* upset with her for some reason. Only she had no idea why or what she could have done. "We're in the cafeteria. Felix said he tried to ring you, but you didn't answer."

That was really the crux of the matter. Why Lucas had failed to answer anyone's calls.

"I forgot to charge my battery after..." He paused, then forged ahead, "I got home. I had to get the extra charger from my vehicle in the car park."

Oh, well, that answered the question about where he'd gone and why he hadn't picked up his mobile. It didn't answer why he was acting the way he was. "Okay. Well, Felix said the child-minder is ill and he had an appointment to keep. He asked if I could watch Cora for a few minutes."

Had Felix not left him a message, like she had?

"I'll be right down to get her."

She tried to smooth things over. "Why don't you join us instead? We're drinking hot chocolate and eating biscuits."

He mumbled something under his breath that she couldn't hear before he came back with, "One of us should stay on the ward."

It was a slow morning and there were several other midwives on duty. Surely he didn't mind sharing her break time?

She simply said, though, "Whatever you think is best. I'll see you when you get here." Then she disconnected before he could say anything else. The last thing she wanted to do was get into an argument with him just when she thought they'd turned a corner.

Turned a corner? Sleeping with him was so much more than that.

Was that what this was all about? Did he suddenly regret what they'd done? Or was he just afraid she was going to become clingy and expect something from him he wasn't willing to give?

She suddenly felt like a fool. Played with and then discarded, like she would have expected him to do with other women. And why *not* her? She was no better than anyone else. Certainly not in Lucas's eyes.

"Darcie, are you okay?" Cora's worried voice broke into her thoughts.

She forced a smile, picking up her hot chocolate and taking a sip of the now-tepid liquid. "Fine. Your uncle is on his way down to have tea with you."

"Shall we order him something, do you think?"

"Oh, I think he can manage that on his own." Another quick smile that made her feel like a total fraud. "And once he gets here I need to get back to work. I have patients that need attending to."

"Can't you stay a little while longer? I know Uncle Luke would want you to."

No, actually he wouldn't. But there was no way she was going to say that to a little girl. "Sorry, love, I wish I could."

The second Lucas arrived Darcie popped up from the table. "See, here she is all safe and sound."

His eyes searched hers for a moment, and she thought she caught a hint of regret in their depths. "I had no doubt she was safe with you."

His hand came out as if to catch her wrist, but Darcie took a step back, going over to Cora and leaning down to kiss the top of her head. "I'm off. Have fun with your uncle."

Then, without a backward glance, she made her way out of the café, wishing she could grind the last fortnight of their rotation into dust and sweep it into the nearest bin.

CHAPTER EIGHT

LUCAS FOUND HER just outside the Teen Mums-to-Be room.

Isla had the door to the tiny conference room open, and she and Darcie were discussing ways to promote the program and give it more visibility. When Isla's eyes settled on him, however, they widened slightly. "I think someone wants to talk to you."

Darcie glanced back, and then her chin popped up, eyes sparkling. "May I help you with something, Mr. Elliot?"

Her sudden formality struck him right between the eyes. He wasn't the only who noticed. Isla looked from one to the other then murmured that she would see Darcie later and left, quietly closing the door behind her.

He'd cursed himself up one side and down the

other for the way he'd spoken to Darcie on the phone yesterday. Margie talking about her miscarriage and wondering if she'd ever be happy again had scrubbed at a raw spot inside him that just wouldn't go away. Because he'd wondered the same thing about his brother time and time again—whether he'd ever be happy again, or if he'd simply wander the same worn paths for the rest of his life or, worse, destroy himself and damage Cora in the process. Love and loss seemed to go hand in hand.

But that had been no reason to take it out on Darcie.

Better make this good, mate.

"I wanted to apologize for being short with you yesterday."

"No need. I should have simply asked your brother to take Cora home when he couldn't reach you, appointment or no appointment. I didn't realize you were so against me spending time with her." Her lips pressed together in a straight line.

She was angry.

And gorgeous. Especially now.

He'd settled Cora in his office yesterday while Felix had gone to his therapy session, and between him and the nurses they'd taken turns keeping her occupied. Every time he'd checked in on her she'd chattered nonstop about Darcie. She'd loaded the pictures from their time at Max's bungee-jumping tower onto his computer. One of those shots had taken his breath away. It had been taken just after he'd unhooked her carabiners, just after he'd kissed her. She'd broken through the surface of the water at the same time as he had, brown hair streaming down her back, fingers clutching his.

And their eyes had been locked on each other. He could only hope none of the nurses had seen the picture.

But in that moment he'd realized why he was so against Darcie and Cora spending time together. Because Darcie was too easy to love. Much like Melody had been.

Cora had already grown attached to the obstetrician. That fact made his chest ache. She'd lost her mother, and very possibly her father. This was one little girl who didn't deserve to experience any more hurt. And she would if he wasn't careful. Because Darcie would be leaving the country. Soon.

He'd tried to apologize to her yesterday, but by the time his brother had come to pick Cora up, Darcie had been flooded with patients and unable to stop and talk. At least, that's what she said. And when their shift had ended, she'd left immediately.

"No, you did the right thing," he said. "I was upset with myself for not getting those calls and leaving you to deal with the whole mess." A partial truth. But if his mobile phone had been charged, he could have avoided all of this.

"Mess?"

Damn, he wasn't explaining himself very well. "Things with my brother are complicated at the moment, and I was worried."

Darcie's brows puckered, but she didn't ask

what the complications were. "It was no problem. Cora and I get on quite well."

"Yes, I've noticed."

If he were smart he'd have let things continue
the way they had yesterday—with Darcie put
out with him—until their rotation ended. But the
note of hurt in her voice, when he'd demanded
to know where Cora was, had punctured something deep inside. He'd found he just couldn't let
her think the worst of him.

Which was why he was here.

She glanced at the door Isla had closed, probably planning her escape. So Lucas blurted out,
"Which thing on your list were you thinking of
tackling next?"

He'd made a promise. He couldn't very well
renege on it, could he? Yes, he damn well could.
He was just choosing not to.

"I hadn't given it much thought today."

He should have said goodbye when he'd woken
up in her bed, but he'd been too damned shocked
to do anything but throw his clothes on and get

out of there. He rarely spent the night at a woman's flat, most of the time leaving soon after the physical act was completed. Because the aftermath always felt uncomfortable. Intimate. And holding a woman for hours after having sex with her? Well, that was something a husband or boyfriend did. Lucas didn't want either of those titles attached to his name.

But he didn't want to hurt anyone unnecessarily either. Especially one who'd already been treated badly by someone else. One he'd promised wouldn't have to accomplish her to-do-while-in-Australia list on her own.

Besides, he'd promised Isla as well.

"How about the pier? We could walk along it tonight, see the moon shining on the water." It had been on the tip of his tongue to suggest a trip to the dock where his sailboat was moored, but he had the same internal rule about that as he did about spending the whole night with a woman. He didn't do it.

"That wasn't on my list."

He offered her a smile. "Maybe lists were made to be changed—added to."

She stared up at him for a long second. "Maybe they were. Okay, Lucas. The pier. Tonight."

Relief swept over him, not only because he wasn't breaking his promise to show her the sights—and the pier at night was one of his favorites—but that she was back to calling him by his first name. He liked the sound of it on her lips.

Especially in that breathy little voice that—

Back to business, Lucas.

"Okay, then, do you want to meet after our shift?"

"Sounds perfect."

Just as Darcie reached for the door handle of the teen mums' room, Tristan Hamilton, MMU's neonatal cardiothoracic surgeon, came sprinting down the hallway. "Flick's in labor."

Isla pushed the door from the other side, making it known that the rooms were not soundproof. "Are you sure?"

Tristan dragged shaky fingers through his hair. "I'm sure. So is she. She knows the signs."

"It's still early." Lucas said what everyone was probably thinking. Heavily pregnant, Tristan's wife had already been through a lot. So had Tristan. The baby had inherited his father's heart defect—a defect that had required Tristan to undergo a heart transplant when he'd been younger. Thankfully, a specialized team had done surgery on the baby in utero a few weeks ago, repairing the faulty organ and inserting a stent, but the baby was still recovering. The fact that Flick had gone into labor wasn't a good sign. It could mean the baby was in distress. A complication from surgery?

He glanced at Darcie, who nodded. "We're on our way."

Isla, the worry evident on her face, said, "I'll come too."

"No." Darcie moved closer and squeezed the other woman's hand. "You're needed here. We'll keep you up to date on what's happening."

"Promise?" Lucas noted Isla's hand had gone to the bulge of her own stomach in a protective gesture he recognized.

"I promise."

Then the trio was off, Tristan leading the pack, while Darcie and Lucas followed behind. Once back on the ward, it was obvious which room Flick was in by the bevy of nurses rushing in and out.

The second they entered the space, Flick—already in a hospital gown—cast a terrified glance their way. "They're coming faster, Tristan. Every two minutes now."

While her husband went to hold her hand, Lucas and Darcie hurriedly washed their hands and snapped on gloves. Lucas nodded at Darcie to do the initial exam while he hooked up the monitor.

Without a word being said, she moved into position. "Tell me if you start contracting, Flick, and I'll stop."

Lucas watched the woman's expression, even

as he positioned the wide elastic band of the monitor around her waist. Once he switched it on the sound of the baby's heart filled the room, along with a palpable sense of relief. No arrhythmias. No dangerous slowing of the heart rate. Just a blessedly normal *chunga-chunga-chunga-chunga* that came from a healthy fetus.

Darcie's face was a study in concentration as she felt the cervix to judge its state. If Flick was still in the early stages of labor, it might be possible to halt it with medication.

Grim little lines appeared around her mouth as she straightened. "Have you noticed any leakage?"

"The baby's been pressing hard on my bladder so…" Her eyes went to her husband. "The amniotic sac?"

Darcie nodded. "It's trickling. And you're at five centimeters and almost fully effaced. There's no stopping it at this point, Flick. Your baby is coming."

"But his heart…"

Tristan, standing beside his wife, looked stunned. "You'd better get Alessandro down here."

The neonatal specialist was in charge of the hospital's NICU. Once the baby was born, Alessandro would make sure everything was working as it should and that the child's tiny heart was okay.

Darcie asked one of the nurses to put in a call, and then she moved up to stroke Flick's head. "It's going to be all right. You're only a few weeks early."

"Mmm…" Flick's blue eyes closed as she pulled air in through her nose and blew out through her mouth. Tristan leaned closer to help her, while Lucas glanced at the monitor. Contraction. Building.

The baby's heart rate slowed as the uterus clamped down further, squeezing the umbilical cord. Everyone held their breath, but the blips on the screen picked up the pace once the contraction crested and the pressure began to ease.

Lucas came over and said in a low voice, "She's going fast for her first."

A few seconds later Alessandro appeared in the room, along with a few more nurses. He studied Flick's chart and then watched the monitor beside the bed for a minute or two. "Let me know when she's getting close. I'll have everything ready."

He shook Tristan's hand. "Congratulations. It looks like you're going to be a daddy today. Have you got a name picked out for her?"

The baby's sex wasn't a secret any more. Tristan and Flick were having a girl.

"We're still having heated discussions about that," Flick said with a shaky smile. "I hoped we'd have a few more weeks to talk it over."

Her husband laid a hand on her cheek. "Let's go with Laura. I know how much you love that name."

"Are you sure?" Tears appeared in her eyes, but then another contraction hit and her thoughts turned to controlling the pain.

Alessandro's attention turned to the monitor to

watch the progression. "Everything looks good so far. Call me when the baby crowns, or if you need me before that." He gave Flick's shoulder a gentle squeeze and then nodded at the rest of them and left the room.

Once labor was in full swing, the room grew crowded with healthcare workers. Flick refused the offer of nitrous oxide, afraid that anything she put into her body at this point would affect the baby, even though the gas was well tolerated and often used to manage labor pain.

"I need to push." Flick's announcement had Darcie at her side in a flash.

She checked the baby's position once again then nodded. "You're all set. Are you ready, Mum?"

"Yes."

They waited for a second as Flick found a comfortable position.

Tension gathered in the back of Lucas's head as he assisted Darcie, while Tristan remained closer to his wife's head, murmuring encouragement.

Lucas saw the climb begin on the monitor.

"Okay, Flick, here it comes, take a deep breath and push."

The woman grabbed a lungful of air, closed her eyes and bore down, helping her contracting uterus do its job. Tristan counted to ten in a slow, steady voice and told her to take another breath and push again.

The pushing phase went as quickly as the rest of the labor had gone. Ten pushes, and Darcie signaled that the baby had crowned. "Someone ring Alessandro."

He must have been close by because he entered the room within a minute and stood at the far wall.

"Here we go, Flick."

Another group of pushes as Darcie guided the baby's shoulders. Then the baby was there, cradled in Darcie's hands. She passed the baby to Lucas, and then worked on suctioning the newborn's mouth and nose, the red scar from surgery still very evident on her tiny chest.

A sharp cry split the air, and Lucas smiled as

bleary, irritated eyes blinked up at him. Laura cried again, waving clenched fists at him and probably everyone else in the room. "Welcome to the world, baby girl," he murmured.

Tristan cut the cord, and then Alessandro took over, carrying the baby over to a nearby table and belting out orders as he listened to the baby's heart and lungs for several long minutes. There was no time for Lucas to worry about that, because they still had the afterbirth to deliver.

A few minutes later baby Laura was placed on Flick's chest with a clean bill of health.

"I don't foresee any problems." Alessandro smiled down at the new parents. "Her heart sounds strong so the surgery was obviously a success."

Flick grabbed her husband's hand, her eyes on his. "See? Don't you start worrying, Tristan. She's fine."

Lucas knew the man had agonized over the baby's health the entire time, but the problem had been caught and corrected early enough to prevent any major damage to her heart. She would need additional surgery as she grew and her veins and arteries matured but, other than that, she had a great prognosis.

Isla stuck her head into the room. "How are they?"

Flick heard her and motioned her in. "See for yourself."

The head midwife crept closer to where Flick was rubbing her baby's back in slow, soothing circles.

"Good on you. She's beautiful, sweetheart. Congratulations."

Alessandro put his arm around his wife's waist, his hand resting on her pregnant belly. "And now we need to let them get to know one another."

As soon as the room had cleared of most of the nurses, and the baby had successfully latched onto Flick's breast, Tristan leaned down and whispered something in his wife's ear that made her smile, although her face bore evidence of her exhaustion.

Lucas's chest tightened. What if all hadn't gone well in here today? What if something had happened to Flick? It was obvious Tristan was deeply in love with her.

His brother's face swam before him. The times he'd drunk himself into a stupor or lain in bed, unwilling to get up and take care of himself or Cora. On days like that it had been left to Lucas to care for them both.

He glanced over at Darcie and found her looking back at him, although her eyes swung away almost immediately. What would it be like to love a woman and not fear she might one day disappear off the face of the planet?

It was better not to even entertain thoughts like that.

Haven't you already?

No.

He and Darcie had been on a few outings. Spent one night together. That did not a relationship make. And if he kept telling himself that, he could make sure it stayed that way.

He glanced at his watch and realized the end of their shift had come and gone. They should have been off duty an hour ago. A deep tiredness lodged in his bones and suddenly all he wanted to do was sit on that pier with Darcie and stare out over the water.

Just for companionship. Just to have someone to share today's victory with.

He walked over to the happy couple. "Do you need anything else? Something to help you sleep?"

"I don't think any of us are going to have trouble in that area." She kissed the top of her baby's head. "Thank you so much for everything."

Tristan echoed that. "I'm going to stay here with them tonight to make sure everything is okay."

And that was their cue to leave. Darcie must have realized it too because she smiled then walked over and kissed Flick on the cheek. "Take care, young lady. Ring if you need anything. You have my mobile number?"

"Yes. Right now, though, all I want to do is watch her sleep."

Lucas followed Darcie out the door and to the nurses' station. "Are we still on for tonight?"

She pushed a lock of hair behind her ear, glancing at the clock. "Do you still want to? It's after nine."

"If you're not too tired. We can get something to eat on the way."

"I'm fine." She hesitated. "As long as you're sure."

Right now, Lucas had never been more sure of anything in his life.

The moon was huge.

Seated on the side of the pier with her legs dangling over the side, Darcie stared out at the light reflected over the water. "I've never seen anything quite like this."

"I know. It's why I enjoy coming out here from time to time."

She cocked her head in his direction. "I should

have made time to do things like this right after I came to Australia. But I wasn't in the mood to do anything besides work."

"Your ex?"

"Yes." This was probably the last thing Lucas wanted to hear while he sat here: her tale of woe. But somehow she found the whole story pouring into the night air. And it felt good. Freeing to actually tell someone besides Isla.

Lucas was silent until she'd finished then said, "Your ex was a bastard. And your maid of honor…well, she wasn't much of a friend, was she?"

She shrugged. Nine and half months had given her enough distance to see the situation more objectively. Yes, Tabitha and Robert could have handled things differently, but it had been better to learn the truth this side of the wedding vows than to have faced the possibility of cheating and a divorce further on down the line. "I think it was hard for both of them. And I don't think they meant to hurt me. That's probably why our engagement continued for as long as it did. But it would have been easier if they'd been honest with themselves…and with me."

"Being honest with yourself doesn't mean you have to act on your impulses."

She frowned. "So you think it would have been better for Robert to go ahead and marry me?"

"No. Maybe it would have been better for him not to become engaged in the first place."

Interesting. She was seeing a new side to Lucas. "Is that comment speaking to my situation? Or do you simply not believe in marriage?"

"It's not so much that I don't believe in it, I'm just apathetic about the whole institution." He leaned back on his hands and stared at the night sky before looking her way again. "But I didn't bring you here to talk about my philosophies on marriage or anything else. I came to enjoy the view."

"I am enjoying it." She took a deep breath, the salty tang that clung to the air filling her senses and rinsing away the stress of the last two days. "It's lovely. You're a very lucky man to be able to come down here whenever you want and take it all in."

"I am a lucky man."

When she turned to glance at him, he was watching her.

"What?" She pulled her cardigan around herself, unsure whether it was because of the slight chill in the air or because he was making her feel nervous.

His brows went up. "Nothing. I'm just taking it all in."

Her? He was taking her in?

A shot of courage appeared from nowhere. "The view's quite good from where I'm sitting as well."

The breeze picked up a bit, and a gust of air flipped her hair across her cheek and into her eyes. She went to push it back, only to find he'd beaten her to it, his hand teasing the errant locks behind her ear. The light touch sent a shiver through her.

His fingers moved to her nape, threading

through the strands there and lifting them so the air currents could pick them up.

Why did everything the man said or did make her insides coil in anticipation? And how could he go from cool and distant to so…here? Present. Insinuating himself into her life and heart in subtle ways that took down all her defenses.

Her mind swept through the events of the day and replayed them. How he'd deferred to her in the delivery room today, letting her take the lead in Flick's delivery while not losing that raw, masculine edge that made him so attractive to her.

And to a thousand other women like her.

Just when she started to thump back to earth his fingers—which were still at the back of her neck—suddenly tangled in her hair, using his light grip to turn her head.

"Your fiancé missed out."

His brown eyes roved over her face, touching on her lips then coming back up. "You're the whole package, Darce. A beauty. Inside and out. And I…"

He let go of her so quickly she had to catch her balance even as he finished his thought, his tone darkening. "And I shouldn't have brought you here."

Where had that come from? One minute he was going on about her hair and how he found her beautiful. The next he was saying he regretted having brought her to the pier.

Hurt—a jagged spear of pain that slashed and tore at everything it came in contact with—caused her voice to wobble. "Then why did you?"

"Because I wanted you to see what I do when I come out to the bay. But all I see right now... is you. And I want to do more than just look."

Everything inside her went numb for a second. Then a swish of realization blew through her, soothing the hurt.

He wanted her. Wanted to touch her. Just like the other night at her flat.

"You can. You can do more."

Before she had time to think or breathe he moved. Fast. His mouth covered hers in a rush of need that was echoed in her. She wanted him. Now. Here. On this pier.

His hand went behind her head as his tongue sought entry. She gave it to him, opening her mouth and letting him sweep inside. He groaned, and the sound was like a balm and a stimulant all at once, although she didn't know how that was possible. Maybe just because of who he was.

Darcie's mouth wasn't the only thing that opened. Her heart did as well, letting him in. Just a crack at first, but then growing wider and wider until he filled her. Surrounded her. Inside and out.

She allowed herself to revel in it, at least for now. Soon she'd have to come back to the real world, but for the moment she would inhabit the land of wish lists and wishful thinking—a place where anything was possible. Where anything could happen.

And, God, she hoped it happened. Soon. Because the need inside her was already too big to be contained.

She pulled back, even though everything was screaming at her to keep going. "Lucas."

"I know." Both hands sank into her hair and he held her still as he ran a line of kisses down her cheekbone, over her jaw, until he reached her ear. "If I don't stop now, I won't."

What? Stop? That's not what she'd meant at all.

"I don't want you to."

A flash of teeth came, followed by, "I don't think you want me to rip your clothes off on a public pier, do you?" A brow lifted. "Unless you're into exhibitionism. Although the thought of having you pressed naked against that bank of windows at your flat—with me inside you— is pretty damned tempting."

Something in her belly went liquid with heat. Not at the thought of exposing herself to thousands of people but at Lucas—inside her.

"My flat is too far away."

He paused for a moment and then stood and held out his hand. "I know the perfect place."

CHAPTER NINE

"I DIDN'T KNOW you had a boat."

No one did. This was the one place Lucas could come that was totally private. Totally his. Where he could get away from the stresses of the day or—when Felix had been in a particularly bad state—the horrors of his own thoughts. The small sailboat had cost him several months' salary, but it had been money well spent. He would live on it were it not for the fact that he needed to be close to the hospital...and to Cora and Felix.

And he'd never brought anyone here...especially not a woman.

So why Darcie?

He stood with her on the deck as the boat swayed at its mooring. Why was this the first place that had come to mind when he'd realized what she wanted?

It was close. And they both wanted sex. It was the obvious choice. Even as he thought it, he knew that wasn't the reason at all.

She was waiting for an answer, though, so he said, "I like the water, and it's nice to have a place where I can enjoy it."

She smiled, leaning against the railing on the far side of the vessel. "I thought that's what the pier was for."

"Sometimes I want a little more privacy." His lips curled, and knowing she'd probably take the words the wrong way he went on, "For myself. Not for any love triangles."

She eased over to him and ran her fingers from the waistband of his jeans up to his shoulders. "I thought we'd already established you don't do any angles at all."

He didn't do a lot of things. But he liked the feel of her hands on him.

Gripping her waist, he dragged her to him, making the boat rock slightly. "So...do you want to stay topside? Or go down below?"

Her brows went up and a choked laugh sounded. "I assume you're not referring to parts of the body."

"No. Because in that I'm definitely an all-inclusive kind of guy." He leaned down and brushed his cheek against hers. "I meant do you want to stay here on deck or go to the cabin?"

"Okay, that makes more sense."

More than once he'd slept beneath the stars on the boat, letting the sounds and movements of the water lull him to sleep. As cool as it was right now, there was no need for air-conditioning.

Darcie glanced at the dock. "Does anyone ever come out here?"

Rows of other boats surrounded them. The small marina was the place of weekend sailors. But in the middle of a workweek? It was always deserted.

"Just me." He smiled, playing on his earlier theme. "Sorry, no one to watch us but the seagulls."

Even in the dark her face flamed. "That's not what I meant."

"Wasn't it?" His hand slid up her side until it covered her breast. The nipple was already tight and ready. "How brave are you feeling, Darcie?"

He tweaked the bud, glorying in the gasp it drove from her throat.

"Right now? Braver than I was during that bungee jump."

"Let's stay out here, then, where we can see the moon."

His hands went to the hem of her cardigan and shirt and swept them over her head, letting the garments drop onto the plank deck. When he touched her arms they were covered in goose bumps, although her skin felt warm. "Are you cold?"

"No." As if in answer, she undid the buttons of his shirt and yanked it from his jeans, helping him tug free from the long sleeves. She tossed it on top of her clothes. The sight stopped him for a second. But just one. Then he was curving his hands behind her back and finding the clasp on her black silk bra. "Last chance to back out, Darcie."

She leaned up and nipped his shoulder. "Just take it off, will you?"

"My pleasure." He unsnapped the bra, and on impulse dangled it over the railing beside them.

Yes, he liked seeing it there, the inky color contrasting with the sleek chrome. It was his declaration to the universe that she was his for tonight. And he knew something else that would look perfect beside it.

He allowed his fingers to trail over the curves he'd exposed. Just for a second, then he released the snap on his jeans and pushed them down his legs, kicking them to the growing pile of clothes beside him. Then he did the same for her. Much slower, kneeling down, so he could savor every inch of her along the way.

Black silk met his eyes. The same color as her bra. He allowed his palms to trail over her hips as he stood, until the slick fabric met the perfect mounds of her ass. He squeezed, pulling her against him and allowing his stiff flesh to imagine that silk sliding over his bare skin.

He had to know. He pulled away, only to have her reach for him. "Just a second, gorgeous. I'm coming right back."

Reaching down to scoop up his jeans, he retrieved a packet from his wallet and set it on the rail next to her bra. Then off came his boxers. His flesh jerked as he drew her back to him.

He closed his eyes as his naked arousal met the silk of her undies. And it was everything he'd imagined. Slick. Arousing. His hands went to her behind and kneaded as he pumped himself against her, slowly, reveling at the contrast between the silky fabric and the warm skin of her belly.

When he felt hands on his own ass, his lids flew apart. "Hell."

He pushed beneath the elastic, and then, unable to wait any longer, he slid her last remaining item of clothing down her hips, waiting until she stepped free before draping it next to her bra.

Mmm…yes. Just like he'd thought. He liked seeing her displayed there. Liked having her on his boat.

Grabbing the condom, he swept a hand beneath her thighs and her shoulders and hauled her into his arms, where he kissed her for what seemed like forever. This time she gave a little shiver, and he noticed the breeze was a bit cooler than it had been on the pier. Still kissing her, he eased to his knees and then lowered her to the deck, her pale skin looking glorious against the shiny teak planks. The raised edges around the deck provided a windscreen, and, balling up their clothing, he lifted her head so she'd have something to cushion it. "Better?"

"It's all good, Lucas. Nothing could be better."

He grinned down at her. "Wanna bet?"

Kneeling between her legs, he sheathed himself, then let his hands move in light, brushing strokes up her inner thighs, until he reached the heart of her. She was already moist and his fingers wanted to linger and explore, but he knew once he let them he was there to stay. And there were other places he needed to visit.

He lowered himself onto her, supporting his weight with his elbows, then murmured against her lips, "Too heavy?"

"Mmm…no. Too perfect."

That made him smile. He didn't think he'd ever heard a woman refer to him that way before. He liked it.

He'd told her the truth earlier. She was gorgeous, inside and out, sporting an inner glow of health and life that made him wonder how he could have ever thought of her as cold.

She didn't feel cold. She felt warm and vital and he itched to lose himself in her all over again.

But first…

He nuzzled the underside of her breast, savoring the taste of her skin as he came up the rounded side and across until he found her nipple. Drawing it into his mouth, he let his tongue play over the peak, hoping to coax the first of those little sounds he knew she made.

And, yes, it was heady being out here in the open, even though he knew no one could see them unless they climbed aboard and walked to the port side of the boat. But the thought that someone could...and that Darcie was letting him love her beneath the stars...was testament to her trust. One he wasn't sure he deserved.

But he liked it.

He applied more suction, and there it was. A low moan that pulled at his flesh and slid along the surface of his mind like a lazy day in the sun. Or maybe it was more like being in the eye of a storm. A fleeting moment of calm, when you sensed chaos lingering nearby...knew you'd soon be swept up in an unstoppable deluge.

And when that happened, he knew right where he wanted to be. And it wasn't pinning her to the deck where he couldn't see or touch.

He pulled back and climbed to his feet, holding his hand out to her.

"Wh-what?"

"Trust me." He picked up his shirt and helped her slide her arms into it, leaving it open in the front and allowing his fingers to dance over her breasts and then move lower. Touching her and relishing the way her eyes closed when he hit that one certain spot.

Putting his forehead to hers, he stopped to catch his breath for a second. "I want you on the railing."

It was the perfect height. She'd be right on a level with that core part of him. And Darcie's silhouette on the water? There was nothing he'd rather see...experience.

She glanced behind her, where her bra and undies were still draped, and backed up until she was against the chrome, her hands resting on the gleaming surface. "Help me up, then."

Gripping her waist, he lifted her onto the rail, his blue shirttail hanging over the other side, giving them a modicum of privacy, although they didn't need it. Her arms twined around his neck and her legs parted in obvious invitation. He moved in, his chest pressing against the lush fullness of her breasts, his flesh aching to thrust home.

"Hang onto me, Darce." Letting go of her waist, he allowed a couple of inches of space to come between them so he could touch her. Her face. Her breasts. Her belly. And finally that warm, moist spot between her legs that was calling out to him.

"Ahhh…" The sound came when he slid a finger inside her, her feet hooking around the backs of his thighs as if she was afraid he was going to move away. Not damn likely. He was there to stay.

His mind skimmed over that last thought. Discarding it as he added another finger. Went deeper. Used his thumb to find that pleasure center just a few millimeters to the front.

Darcie leaned further back over the side of the boat, her hands going to his shoulders, her legs parting more. This time Lucas was the one who groaned. Splayed out like this, he could see every inch of her, watch the way her breasts moved in time to his fingers as he pressed home and then pulled back.

"Want you. Inside…" The words were separated by short, quick breaths. She was getting close. So very close.

And he didn't want her to go off without him.

There it was. The same sense of need he'd had the last time they'd been together. He moved into position and guided himself home. Paused. Then he thrust hard. Sank deep. His breath shuddered out then air flooded back into his lungs.

Tight. Wet. Hot.

All the things he knew she'd be.

And it was all for him.

He held himself still as she whimpered and strained against him. It wouldn't take much to send him over the edge. He counted. Prayed. Closed his eyes. Until he could take a mental step back.

Only then did he wrap his arms beneath the

curve of her butt to hold her close. He eased back, pulling almost free. Remained there for an agonizing second or two before his hips lunged forward and absorbed the sensations all over again. Over and over he drove himself inside her and then retreated.

He leaned forward. Bit her lower lip. Made her squirm against him.

"Please, Lucas. Please, now."

He knew exactly what she was asking for. "Make it happen, gorgeous."

Changing the angle, he reconnected with her, then pushed deep and held firm as she ground her pelvis against him, letting her choose her own speed, her own pressure, all the while cursing in his head as his eyes reopened to watch her face—taking in the tiny, almost desperate bumping of her hips.

His hands tightened on her, barely aware that the vibrations from their movements had sent her undies over the rail and into the water, and that her bra wasn't far behind. He didn't care. Didn't want to stop for anything.

Legs wrapped tight around him, Darcie's movements became frantic, nails digging into his shoulders…for all of five seconds—he knew because he was busy counting—then her head tilted toward the sky, hair streaming down her back, and she cried out in the darkness.

That was it. All it took. Lucas pumped furiously as the tsunami he'd been holding at bay crashed down on top of him. He lost himself in her, legs barely supporting his weight as he rode out his climax, knowing a tidal wave of another kind was not far behind. Coming on him fast.

He stared straight ahead so he wouldn't have to see it, wouldn't have to acknowledge its existence, and found her watching him, her gaze soft and warm.

Accepting.

At that moment the second realization hit him, splashing over his head and making it impossible to breathe. To think.

He loved her.

In spite of everything he'd been through with his brother. In spite of the dangers of letting himself get too close—too emotionally involved— the unthinkable had just become reality. He'd fallen for a woman. And now that he had, there wasn't a damned thing he could do about it.

She could only avoid him for so long.

Two days had passed, and she was still reeling from what they'd done on Lucas's boat. How he'd buttoned her into her cardigan and slacks—her undergarments nowhere to be found—probably resting on the bottom of the boat slip, waiting on some unsuspecting soul to find them when it was daytime. Mortified, she made Lucas promise he'd go back and see if he could locate them— hoping her argument against pollution had been convincing enough.

They'd been in her locker the next day—how he'd known the combination she had no idea, but she was thankful no one had to see him handing her the plastic bag that contained her errant underwear.

If anything, though, it made her feel even more embarrassed. How had he found them? A net? A gaff from his boat? Or had they just been floating on the surface of the water, trapped between his boat and the dock?

That thought made heat rush into her face. She picked up her pace as she went down the hallway toward the double glass doors of the waiting room, which swished open as soon as she got close. She was supposed to meet Isla for lunch.

But when she arrived she saw her friend deep in conversation with Sean Anderson. Oh, no. Surely he wasn't giving her a hard time again about Isabel. She sped up even more and arrived in time to hear her ask if he'd heard from her sister. The opposite of what Darcie had expected to hear.

"No. And I'm not sure I want to, at this point."

"Really?" her friend asked, giving Darcie a

quick glance. "After all that, you're just giving up?"

"I don't know. But I do want some answers. And I don't think I'm going to get them here."

"I'm sorry, Sean. I wish I could help."

Darcie decided to speak up. "Maybe you should consider going to the source."

"Funny you should say that," Sean said. "I decided to take Isla's advice. My contract runs out at the end of the week. I'm flying out as soon as it does."

The two women looked at each other, and Darcie's heart began to thump. Maybe she couldn't fix her own growing problems with Lucas, but maybe Sean could solve his. "So you're going..."

Sean nodded. "To England."

Isla clasped her hands over her belly, knuckles white. "Don't hurt her. Please. You have no idea what she's been through."

"I have no intention of hurting anyone. All I want is the truth about why she left."

Her friend studied him then reached out and

touched his arm. "Good luck, Sean. I really mean that."

"Thanks." And with a stiff frame and tight jaw he strode down the hallway toward an uncertain future.

Well, join the club. Who really knew what the future held. Certainly not Darcie, who was busy hiding out and praying that Lucas gave her some time to recover. She needed to figure out what it was she wanted from him before he suggested tackling the next thing on her list.

Because that list had begun to revolve around a common theme, one that was getting her in deeper with each item ticked: Sit on a beach and kiss an Aussie. Bungee jump from a tower and kiss an Aussie. Dance at a club, and make love to an Aussie. Climb on a boat…and open her heart to an Aussie.

Darcie didn't know how much more she could take. Because her heart was now in real danger, and she was more afraid than she'd ever been in her life…even during that moment when she'd realized Robert didn't love her. He loved someone else.

Because if that happened with Lucas, she didn't want to stick around to see it. The result would be a gaping wound no amount of surgery or medical expertise could repair. It involved who she was at an elemental level. And in opening her heart she feared she'd set herself up for the biggest hurt of her life.

Isla said something, and Darcie swung her attention back to her friend. "I'm sorry. I missed that."

The midwife smiled. A quick curving of lips that looked all too knowing and crafty. "I said, don't look now, but trouble is headed your way."

That was the understatement of the year. Then she realized Isla's eyes were on something behind her.

Darcie turned to look, thinking one of her patients was coming to see her, only to catch sight of the same glass doors she'd just come through swishing open to let in the last person she wanted to see today.

Lucas.

He looked devastating in a dress shirt and black slacks. Her glance went back to the shirt. Blue button-down.

Oh, no. Surely that wasn't the shirt he'd draped around her while they'd...

Warmth splashed into her face and ran down her neck, spreading exponentially the closer he got.

"Hello, ladies."

Instead of sweeping past and continuing on his way, he stopped in front of them.

Isla's smile grew wider. "Darcie, I think I'm going to have to back out of our lunch date. I need to see Alessi about...tires for his car."

Tires? For his car?

Before she could call her friend on the obvious fib, Isla had retreated back through the doors, leaving her with Lucas and a few folks in the waiting room, who seemed quite interested in the various dramas unfolding in the MMU.

As if he'd noticed as well, he pulled her over to the far wall, well out of earshot. "Felix and Cora are on their way to the park with a picnic lunch. It's not far from the hospital, so I thought you might like to tag along. It's something you should see before you leave the country."

Leave the country. Why did that have an ominous ring to it?

Lucas went on, "From what Isla said, I take it you haven't eaten yet."

Rats. That would have been her first excuse if he approached her. It was why she'd practically begged Isla to have lunch with her for the last two days. And now her friend had turned traitor and abandoned her.

Her eyes met Lucas's face. He seemed softer all of a sudden. As if the weight of the world had been lifted from his shoulders. But what weight? Maybe he was just happy to be having lunch with his niece and his brother. It was obvious he loved that little girl and that she adored him back.

As if sensing her hesitation, he added, "Cora would love to see you. She's been asking about you for days."

Well, that was a change. Before, he hadn't seemed keen on her spending time with his niece.

Her heart settled back in place. The comment about leaving Australia hadn't meant anything. "I guess it would be all right."

"I'm glad." One finger came out and hooked around hers and the side of his mouth turned up in way that made her stomach flip. "Did you get my little package?"

He was definitely in a cheerful mood today. Did she dare hope it was because of the time they'd spent together over the last three weeks? How strange that something she'd dreaded with every fiber of her being could have turned around so completely.

She decided to add some playfulness of her own. "Little? I thought the package was a decent size. But, then again, I don't have much to compare it to."

"Witch," he murmured. "Maybe you need a refresher. It has been a couple of days after all."

A refresher? He wanted to be with her again?

Maybe she wouldn't wind up on the hurting side of the fence after all. As long as she was careful. And took things slowly. She'd been thinking about seeing if the Victoria had any permanent positions available, but she'd been putting it off because of Lucas. She didn't want to stick around if they were going to end up fighting each other further on down the line.

But right now she didn't see that happening.

"Maybe I've just forgotten." She threw him a saucy smile.

"Mmm…I need to work harder next time, then, to make sure that doesn't happen." The finger around hers gave a light squeeze. "Meet you in the car park in fifteen minutes? I have one more patient to schedule, and then I'll be free."

"Okay," she said. Her spirits soared to heights

that were dizzyingly high. A fall from up here could…

She wasn't going to fall. For the first time in a long time she caught a glimpse of something she hadn't expected to feel.

Hope.

Pete the Geek was on a rampage.

Reclining on the blanket that Darcie had somehow scrounged up, Lucas lay on his back, hands behind his head as he watched his niece chasing the dog around their little area of the park. Pete never went far, but seemed intent on having his little bit of fun on this outing, since the cold packed lunch hadn't been on the menu for him.

Darcie sat next to Lucas's shoulder and laughed as Cora just touched Pete's collar, only to have him leap out of reach once again. "He has his timing down to a science, doesn't he?"

"He does at that." He couldn't resist taking one of his hands from behind his head and resting it just behind Darcie's bottom. No one could see.

But he just needed to touch her. Not in a sexual sense, although that always hovered in the background where this woman was concerned. But he found he wanted that closeness in more areas. Just for now. In a very little while she would be gone, and while there might be pain in letting her go, at least she would be alive. It wouldn't be like losing someone to death. He could accept loving her within those parameters.

He'd warred with himself for the last two days but had come up with a compromise he hoped he could live with. He would let himself go with the flow. For the next couple of months.

She sent him a smile in response.

Warm contentment washed through him. Maybe this was why Felix had gone so far off the rails after losing Melody. Lucas had never felt like this about a woman. He loved her. He no longer even tried to deny it. And after staying away from her for two days he'd found he was miserable—and he'd had to find her. Be with her.

For the next two months.

He found himself sending his subconscious little memos. Just so it wouldn't forget. This was a temporary arrangement.

Felix seemed better. His therapy was evidently kicking in. He was fully engaged in what Cora was doing with Pete, really laughing for the first time in years. "Maybe if you tempt him with the ball?"

Cora spun back toward them, while Darcie held out the ball that had landed near her hip a while ago. Leaning down, the little girl flung her arms around Darcie's neck and popped a kiss on her cheek. "I'm so glad you came!"

"I'm glad I did too."

Lucas tensed for a second then forced himself to relax. Darcie and Cora could still keep in contact, even after she flew back to England. There was email and all kinds of social networks. It wouldn't be a drastic break. Just one that would fade away with time.

His niece rushed off with the ball in hand and threw it hard toward Pete, who loped off after the offering with a bark of happiness, scooping it up in his jaws and trotting back toward the blanket.

Lucas smiled and shook his head, his attention going back to Felix.

Only his brother wasn't watching Cora any more. His gaze was on Lucas, his eyes seeming to follow the line of his arm to where it disappeared behind Darcie's back.

Swallowing, he returned his hand to behind his head, and then as an afterthought sat up completely. Darcie glanced at him, head tilted as if she was asking a question. Swamped by a weird premonition, he got to his feet and slapped his brother's shoulder, urging him to come with him to help Cora round up the dog and bring him back to the picnic area.

He watched Felix as they worked, but whatever he thought he'd seen in his brother's face was no longer there. Felix smiled and joked and was finally the one to grab hold of Pete the Geek's collar and snap the leash onto it. Once they were all back at the picnic area he saw that Darcie had packed everything up and was on her feet. "I probably need to get back to the hospital."

That uncertainty he'd caught in her expression from time to time was back.

Because of him.

This was ridiculous. He was imagining demons where none existed. Probably excuses created in the depths of his own mind. There was no reason history had to repeat itself. "I do too. I'll walk you." On impulse, he leaned down and kissed her cheek, watching as they turned that delicious shade of pink he loved so much.

He turned back to say goodbye to Cora, noting his brother's eyes were on him again. He returned the look this time. "Everything okay?"

"Yep. I need to get Cora home so Chessa doesn't worry. Besides, I have some drawings I need to get to."

Felix had once been a respected architect. When he'd married Melody he kept on working, even though she'd been wealthy enough that he hadn't had to. He'd inherited a fortune after she'd died, but it had meant nothing to him. He'd withdrawn from work and every other area of his life, including Cora. It made Lucas's heart a little bit lighter to see him showing an interest in something he'd once been so passionate about.

"Anything interesting?"

"I don't know yet. I'll have to wait and see what it looks like before I decide."

Kind of like Lucas himself? Waiting to see what things with his brother looked like before going on with his life?

Maybe. He wasn't sure. He still hadn't sorted it all out in his head, but he knew he wanted to spend more time with Darcie. Both during their rotation and after it was over.

For how long? Until she left for England?

He slung an arm around her waist, no longer certain of that, despite his earlier lecture. That drawing hadn't been completed yet. Maybe, like Felix, he should wait to see how things shaped up before deciding things like that.

Felix's eyes were on them again, although a

smile stretched his lips. "I'll see you tomorrow, then, right?"

"Definitely." He walked over and kissed the top of Cora's head then ruffled the fur behind Pete's ears. "Be good, you guys."

"We will, won't we, Pete?"

Lucas gave his brother a half-hug. "You'll be okay taking them home?"

"Of course. I wouldn't have brought them otherwise." His brother's voice was just a little sharper than he'd expected, and Lucas took the time to really look at him. Felix's skin was drawn tight over his cheeks, but he still had that same smile on his face. Maybe he was just tired. He hadn't done outings like this in years. Lucas couldn't expect him to spring from point A to point B in the blink of an eye. It was better not to push for more until his brother was ready.

Just in case, he didn't put his arm back around Darcie's waist. That could wait until his brother and Cora were in the car and out of sight. Besides, he didn't want them to witness him kissing the living daylights out of her right there in the park. Which he intended on doing. Then they could go back to work and act like nothing had ever happened. And hopefully Darcie would be amenable to him driving her home afterward. Enough so that she'd ask him up for coffee?

His brother loaded everything in the car. Cora gave one last wave before she got in and they drove away.

Taking hold of Darcie's hips, he tugged her close.

She grinned up at him. "You know, I think *you* might be the one with exhibitionist tendencies, not me."

"Where you're concerned, anything's possible." With that, he proceeded to do what he'd said he was going to and slanted his mouth over hers, repeating the act until she was clinging to him, and until he was in danger of really showing the world what he felt for this woman. "Time to get back to work."

Her mouth was pink and moist, and her eyes

held a delicious glazed sheen. He'd put that there. And he intended to keep it there for as long as possible all through the night.

And then he was going to invite her to come to dinner with him at Felix and Cora's house tomorrow evening. They wouldn't mind, especially since he was the one doing the grilling.

After that? He wrapped his arm around her waist and walked with her the rest of the way to the hospital.

He'd have to see what the drawing looked like further on down the road, but he could afford to give it a little more time to take shape. At least for now.

CHAPTER TEN

LUCAS WASN'T AT WORK.

Darcie did her rounds, trying not to think the worst. He'd been fine at the picnic yesterday. And he'd spent most of last night at her place, making love to her with an intensity and passion that had taken her breath away. After several different places and positions, he'd finally groaned and dragged himself from beneath her covers. "I need to get home so I can be at work on time tomorrow morning." He leaned over and rested his arms on either side of her shoulders, bracketing her in and swooping down for another long kiss. "My rotation partner is a slave driver. She gets all put out when I come in rumpled, wearing the same clothes I had on the day before."

"Maybe that's when she thought you were involved with all sorts of different women."

He'd laughed. "How disappointing it must be to find out what a square I actually am."

"Just the opposite. I was jealous of the way the patients in the MMU always seem to fawn over you. I just wouldn't admit it to myself."

With a laugh, he'd scooped her up and kissed her shoulder. "See you in the morning, gorgeous."

That had been the last she'd heard from him.

She'd walked on cloud nine as she'd got ready for work. Then, when she arrived, she eagerly waited for him to make an appearance and toss her one of those secretive smiles she was coming to love.

But there'd been nothing. No phone calls. No text messages. And nothing on the board to show his schedule had been changed.

Surely he'd made it home safely.

And even though he hadn't said the words, he had to care about her. The way he'd touched her at the park and put his arm around her in full view of his brother and niece had said he wasn't embarrassed to be seen with her.

She cringed at that thought. That was something the Darcie of old would have worried about. Her experience with Robert had shaken her confidence in herself as a woman to the very core. Lucas was slowly building it back up. Kiss by kiss. Touch by touch. He acted like he couldn't get enough of her.

Well, the feeling was mutual.

Today she was not going to let his tardiness get the better of her. She was going to simply enjoy what they'd done last night and not worry about anything else. He'd eventually turn up. He'd probably stopped in to see Cora or something. Or maybe he'd had to drive her to school, which he'd said he'd done on occasion.

He wasn't in bed with someone else. Of that she was sure. Because she was feeling the effects of his loving this morning. It was a delicious ache that reminded her that, no matter who fluttered their lashes at him, Lucas had chosen her.

She sighed and glanced at her watch again. An hour and no word. There was nothing to do but go on with her day and not worry about it. She was tempted to ring his mobile, but was afraid that might seem desperate or needy. So she let it go.

The morning continued to race by at a frenetic pace. Then one o'clock came with no time to break for lunch. She'd just completed one delivery and was heading for the next laboring patient when she saw Isla at the nurses' station. She hurried over.

"Have you heard from Lucas? Or do you know if he's arrived at work yet? I haven't seen him all day."

Her friend blinked at her for a second and then her eyes filled with something akin to horror. "Oh, sweetheart, you haven't heard?"

Only then did she see that Lucas's name had been crossed off today's rota and Isla's name was written in instead. That had to have been done after she'd looked at it this morning.

Darcie's vision went dark for a second or two. "Heard what?"

"Oh…I'm so sorry. I got a call around an hour ago, asking me to step in." She reached out and gripped her hand. "Lucas is in the emergency department…"

Isla's voice faded out in a rush of white noise but the words "alcohol poisoning" and "gastric lavage" came through, before a nurse came out of the room of her next patient. "Mrs. Brandon is feeling the urge to push, and she's panicking. She isn't listening to instruction, Dr. Green."

Somehow, Darcie managed to stumble into the room, and despite her clanging heart she was able to coax the nitrous mouthpiece from between the woman's clamped jaws and get her to focus on pushing at the appropriate times. The baby was a large one, and Darcie had to do some fancy maneuvering to get the baby's shoulders through the narrow space. Then he was out and wailing at the top of his lungs. Darcie wished she could drop onto the nearest chair and join him for a hearty cry. But she couldn't. And it was another hour of praying for a break before one finally came and she could make her way down to Emergency.

Her heart was in her throat. Lucas had alcohol poisoning? How could that be? She'd never seen him touch a drop of the stuff, except for the sips she'd talked him into taking of her drink. And he'd made the most godawful face once he had. She'd convinced herself he was a teetotaler, that he just didn't like alcohol. But maybe she'd got it all wrong. Maybe he was a recovering alcoholic. Or, worse, one who binge-drank for seemingly no reason.

But alcohol poisoning was more than just a couple of drinks. It was a life-threatening toxic buildup that came from downing one drink after another without giving the liver time to filter the stuff out of the blood.

Why hadn't Isla come back to find her as soon as she'd heard the news?

Maybe because she'd been just as swamped as Darcie had been—and just as exhausted. She saw on the patient board that the letters "TMTB" had been scrawled beside two of the names, so her friend had to have been run ragged with those girls—and with all the aftercare that went along with teen pregnancies.

She paused just outside the doors to the emergency department, unsure what she was going to find. Isla would have surely told her if Lucas was in danger of dying, wouldn't she? Maybe the stomach pumping had done its job and he was already on the road to recovery. Maybe he was simply too ashamed to face her.

As well he should be.

Anger crawled through her veins, pushing aside the worry and fear. If he were an alcoholic, shouldn't he have told her? Refused that offer of a drink she'd given him?

A thought spun through her brain. What if that sip had sent him over the edge? An alcoholic shouldn't drink *any* type of liquor. Ever.

All those late mornings…the rumpled clothes. The surly demeanor when he finally arrived.

God.

She squared her shoulders and stepped on the mat that would open the glass doors and went through. Noise and shouting hit her. The place was just as busy as the MMU had been. Making her way over to the desk and hoping to find a nurse or someone who could provide her with information, she searched the patient board for a familiar name.

Out of the corner of her eye she caught sight of him.

Lucas.

He was on his feet, leaning against a wall. She'd recognize those broad shoulders and wavy hair anywhere. But he didn't look right. He was slumped, leaning against the flat surface as if he could barely hold himself up.

The waiting room was crowded, but surely he'd been seen already. Alcohol poisoning was normally run up to the top of the list. Could Isla have exaggerated or made a mistake?

At that moment his eyes met hers.

And what was in them tore apart any thought

of exaggeration. There was torment and pain in that red, bleary gaze.

So much pain.

Hurrying over, she stopped next to him.

"Lucas, what's wrong? Are you ill?" she asked.

He didn't answer, just shook his head. His hair was tousled, and two of the bottom buttons of his shirt were undone, as if he'd thrown himself together in a rush.

"I don't understand. Isla said something about alcohol poisoning. She wasn't talking about you?"

"No." Lucas's hands fisted at his sides. "Did you think she was?"

"I didn't know what to think." Confusion swirled around her head. Why did he seem so angry?

"It's not me. It's my brother."

"Felix?" The sound of a siren drowned out his response as an ambulance pulled up to the front entrance. The sound of slamming doors came and then a gurney rushed in with a patient who was obviously in bad shape from the number of healthcare staff heading toward him. When she could finally be heard again she asked, "What happened?"

Two seats opened up as a couple with a child were called back to one of the exam rooms.

She took his hand to lead him over to the chairs so he could sit down before he fell down. He tugged free of her grip but followed her over to the seats. A chill went through her that had nothing to do with Felix's condition as they both sat.

"What happened to Felix?"

He propped his elbows on his knees and stared at the ground. Without looking at her, he said, "He drank himself into a stupor."

"Oh, no." So it was alcohol poisoning. Isla had been right about that. "What about Cora?"

He gave a mirthless laugh. "She's the one who rang me this morning. Felix was out all night, and when he finally made it home he collapsed in the foyer. Chessa had to spend the night at the house because she couldn't reach me. And so here I am."

Her heart squeezed tight. They hadn't been able to reach him because he'd been at her house until almost three that morning, his mobile and car keys deposited on her entry table. "I'm so sorry, Lucas. Will he be okay?"

"I don't know. He may be too far gone this time."

This time?

Things fell into place in the blink of an eye. This was why Felix had seemed off when she'd met him those weeks ago—why he and Lucas had argued. He was the alcoholic, not Lucas.

"He seemed fine at the park."

"He was." Lucas lifted his head long enough to glance in her direction. "At least I thought he was."

That explained something else. Lucas had seemed light and happy. Happier than she'd ever known him to be. She'd assumed it had been because of their budding relationship. But maybe that hadn't been the case at all. Maybe it had been because his brother had been doing so well.

Maybe all those affectionate touches and looks had been spillover from what had been going on with Felix.

And last night? Had that simply been an overflow of happiness as well?

Her brain processed another fragment. He hadn't rung her to tell her where he was this morning. Or that his brother was in trouble. He—or someone—had notified Isla instead.

Maybe he hadn't wanted to worry her.

But surely he knew she'd be frantic when he didn't show up for work.

Her thoughts spiraled down from there. He hadn't bothered to tell her the truth about his brother's condition. Or what he'd been dealing with for who knew how long. He'd led her to believe things were fine. With Felix and Cora.

With her.

Just like Robert had done.

When trouble had come to visit, she'd been the last one to find out—and the result had been devastating.

You're jumping to conclusions, Darcie. Give the man a chance to explain.

Only he didn't. He just sat there. She'd had to drag every piece of information out of him the entire time she'd known him. Was this what she wanted? A lifetime full of secrets? Of wondering if things were okay between them?

No.

Something inside her wouldn't let her give up quite so easily, though. Not without trying one last time to reach him.

"He'll be okay." She knew the reassurance was empty. She had no idea exactly how bad things were. Only Lucas and the doctors knew how much liquor he'd ingested or how much damage had been done to his liver and other organs.

"Will he?"

"What did the doctors say?" She had to keep pushing. To see if he was worth fighting for.

Because she loved him.

Oh, God, she loved him, and she didn't want

to have to let him go, unless there was no other option.

"They pumped his stomach. Rehydrated him with fluids and electrolytes. I just have to wait for him to wake up."

She didn't understand. "Will they not let you back to see him?"

"I needed to think about some things. I'll go back in a little while."

"And Cora?"

"She's still with Chessa. We both thought it best not to have her here until we knew something definitive. She's already lost her mum. I don't want her to panic over what might happen to her dad. Unless it actually does."

"It might not come to that." She licked her lips and got up the nerve to slide her hand over his. This time he didn't shake her off. But he also didn't link his fingers through hers or make any effort to acknowledge the contact. "Is there anything I can do to help?"

"If he makes it, he'll have to go to rehab. A residential one this time. I can't trust him to care for Cora at this point."

Which was why he'd been late those other times. Another piece fell into place.

He'd had to take care of his niece when his brother had been too sick or too drunk. And what had she done? She'd yelled at him in front of a roomful of people on one of those days. Guilt washed over her, pummeling her again and again for assuming things that hadn't been true. For not asking him straight out if something was wrong. Maybe she could have helped somehow.

Maybe she still could.

"If you need me to watch Cora, I—"

"No." The word was firm. Resolute. "We'll be fine."

Another chill went through her, and the premonition she'd had earlier came roaring back to haunt her.

He was still going to pretend that things were okay—shutting her out without a moment's hesitation. She removed her hand from his and curled it in her lap.

Lucas sat up, his mouth forming a grim line. "I think I'm going to take some personal time. I have Cora to think about, and I'll need to deal with Felix. I can't do that and work at the same time."

Her heart stalled. "How will you live?"

"I have some savings. And Cora's care comes from a trust fund her mother left for her."

"I see." She licked her lips. "How much time are we talking?"

"A couple of months at the very least. Maybe more." He didn't skip a beat. He'd obviously already thought this through.

She did the calculations and a ball of pain lodged in her chest. He'd be out until after she left Australia and headed back to England. Surely he couldn't mean to drop out of her life as quickly as he'd come into it. Not after everything that had happened between them.

"I could come by after work, help with the cooking."

"I think it would be better if you didn't, Darcie. Please. For everyone's sake."

For everyone's sake. Whose, exactly? His?

"I don't understand."

"Felix is here because he can't get over the death of his wife, despite years of therapy. When he saw you and I together at the park…" He shrugged. "You knew there was never going to be anything permanent between us. At least I thought you did. And right now I have to think about what's best for my family."

His eyes were dull and lifeless. So much so that it made her wonder if he even knew how much he was hurting her with his words.

Then he looked at her, and she saw the truth. He knew. He just didn't care.

The ball grew into a boulder so big she could barely breathe past it. He was dumping her. His brother's illness provided the perfect excuse.

Only, like her ex-fiancé, he didn't have the decency to come to her and tell her until it was as obvious as the nose on her face.

Well, that was okay. She'd survived being jilted at the altar, so she could survive the breakup of something that amounted to a few nights of sex and adventure. He'd wanted to do some wild and outrageous stuff? Well, she'd done enough to last a lifetime. And she didn't have it in her to stick around and watch her world fall apart piece by piece.

One thing she *could* do was make this final break as easy as possible for the both of them. "I'm truly sorry about Felix, and I hope everything works out with him. But if your decision to leave the MMU has anything to do with me or the time we spent together, this should put your mind at ease. I've decided to go back to England early."

He eyed her for several long seconds before saying, "When did you decide this?"

Right now. Right this second. When I realized I'm good enough to warm your bed at night but not good enough to take up permanent residence in your heart—to share your joys and heartaches.

But she couldn't say that. Not unless she wanted the remnants of her shattered pride to fall away completely and expose everything she'd hoped to hide.

Then the perfect response came to her in a flash, and she snatched at it, before taking a deep breath and looking him straight in the eye. "I decided last night."

CHAPTER ELEVEN

ISLA SLAMMED OPEN the door to his office, green eyes flashing. "What did you do to Darcie?"

Lucas hadn't seen her for the last two days, so he'd assumed she'd already flown home. In fact, that was why he was still at work, tying up loose ends, albeit with shorter hours. Chessa was staying with Cora during the day, and at night he went and slept on the couch.

Felix was still in the hospital, but he was slowly regaining his strength. His brother had admitted what Lucas knew in his heart to be true. That seeing him and Darcie together had reopened wounds that had scabbed over but never fully healed.

And what about Darcie?

He'd hurt her, but he hadn't known what else to do. His brother's life was at stake—because of something he'd done. He couldn't let that happen again.

Besides, hadn't he seen time and time again how love brought you to the brink of disaster and sometimes tossed you over the edge? Everything he'd seen lately had reinforced that. Margie's miscarriage. Tristan and Flick almost losing their baby. His brother almost losing his life.

Isla crossed her arms over her chest, clearly waiting for him to answer her.

"Thank you for knocking before you burst in." When the jibe earned him nothing but a stony stare he planted both his hands on his desk. "I didn't do anything to her, Isla. She said she decided to go back to England earlier than planned."

"Why? Did you sleep with her?"

Hell, if the woman wasn't direct. "I don't see that that's any of your business."

"Maybe not. But I think she was right about you. You're nothing but an arrogant, self-righteous bastard who thinks he can sit above all of us and not dirty his hands with real life and real love. I know…because my husband was once just like you."

"She said that about me?" He tried to ignore the hit to his gut that assessment caused. "As for Alessandro, I bet he didn't have a drunken brother to contend with. Or a niece who needed him."

"And that justifies you hurting Darcie?"

No. Nothing justified that. And he would be damned every moment of his life for what he'd done. But she'd said she was going to leave anyway.

It was a lie, you idiot. You'd practically hung a do-not-disturb sign on your heart and dared anyone to knock. And then once she did, you slammed the door in her face.

Because of Felix.

Really?

Was it because his brother had relapsed—which he'd done on several other occasions without any help from him—or was it because he was too afraid to "dirty his hands", as Isla claimed.

He'd once sat on a beach and dared Darcie to do something wild and outrageous. And she'd risen to the challenge and beyond. And yet here he sat, too afraid to make a list of his own because "loving Darcie" would be at the top of it.

He was terrified of holding his hand out to her for fear of losing her. And the thought of becoming like his brother—a shell of a man...

But what about what Isla had asked? Did any of that excuse what he'd done to Darcie? Because of his own selfish fear?

"No," he said. "It didn't justify it."

Isla seemed to lose her steam. "I didn't expect you to agree with me quite so quickly."

"I know what I did. And I'm not proud of it." If he had it to do all over again, would he? He'd made an impulsive decision while his brother had been fighting for his life—a huge mistake, according to the experts. He should have given himself a day or two before deciding something that would affect both of their lives.

The memory of her laughter, those pink-cheeked smiles…that raw sincerity when she'd offered to help with Cora's care. He'd thrown it all away. He hadn't given a thought to how she might have felt, or how right it seemed to be with her. He'd only thought of himself. And in that process he'd done to her what he'd been so afraid might happen to him. He'd abandoned her. Left her standing all alone.

"Isla, you're a genius. And I'm a fool." He got up and went around the desk and planted a kiss right on her forehead.

Her face cleared, and she laughed. "I won't tell Alessi you did that. He might knock your teeth right out of your head."

"He knows you're crazy about him…and the whole world knows how he feels about you."

"True. So what are you doing to do about all this other stuff?" She rolled her hand around in the air.

What *was* he going to do? He'd run Darcie off and it wasn't like he could do anything about it. He was here. Having to make sure his brother made it in to rehab as soon as he was released from the hospital. He couldn't just hop on the first flight to England and leave Cora by herself. He was stuck.

"I don't know, actually. I have responsibilities here."

Her mouth curved into a half-smile. "Isn't it lucky, then, that Alessi loves me as much as you say he does?"

Lucas had no idea what that had to do with anything. "Yes, I guess it's lucky for you."

"And for you too. Because he happens to know someone high up at the airline Darcie was scheduled to fly on."

He only caught one word of that whole spiel. "Was?"

"It seems her flight was overbooked, and she was booted to one that leaves tomorrow afternoon."

Hope speared through him, causing him to drop back into his chair. "She's still in Melbourne?"

"For another day. Yes."

"Why the hell didn't you say something before now?"

"Because I wasn't sure you loved her enough to fight for her. And if you don't, she deserves better."

He swallowed. She deserved better anyway. Better than that bastard ex of hers. Better than *him*. "You're right. I'm not good enough for her."

"I might have agreed with you a few minutes ago but I saw your face when the enormity of what you'd done hit you. You were frantically trying to figure out a way to make it right…to get to her. Well, Alessi and I have just given it to you. Don't waste it, Lucas. Because by tomorrow afternoon she'll be gone, and it'll be too late."

He got to his feet. "If she's gone, it'll be because she doesn't want me. Because as of right now I'm going to fight for her with everything I have in me and hope to God she'll forgive me."

Darcie wandered through the empty flat, which was in much the same state as when she'd arrived. There were suitcases sitting neatly side by side, and in her purse was a one-way ticket. She'd come here looking to escape a painful past, only to end up fleeing a new situation that was even worse.

Her feelings for Lucas were light years beyond the ones she'd had for Robert, which maybe explained why he'd found her lacking that certain spark. She had. It had taken Lucas to put a match to it and bring it to life.

Only he'd evidently felt even less for her than her ex had. Because he'd made no pretense of loving her or even wanting a long-term relationship with her. Hadn't he told her that in plain English at the very beginning, when he'd first suggested putting pen to paper and making that list?

She gave a pained laugh. "He did, but you just couldn't accept that, could you? You had to fall in love with the man, didn't you?"

A knock sounded at the door and Darcie froze, wondering if someone had heard her. The doorman was supposed to ring the interphone if she had a visitor. Her heart thumped back to normal. It was probably just the taxi. She'd asked the airport to send someone if they found her an earlier flight. The sooner she was out of Melbourne the better.

She felt like such a fool and every second she stayed in this flat—in this country—was a horrid reminder of how she'd practically groveled at the man's feet, only to have him knock her offer aside and ask her to leave him alone.

Which was what she was trying to do.

She scrubbed her palms under her eyes, irritated that she had turned into the weepy female she'd vowed never to be again.

Hauling her suitcases to the front door, she went back for her purse and opened the door. "Do you mind getting those? I…"

It took three or four blinks before she realized the man standing at the door wasn't a taxi driver. Or the doorman.

It was Lucas.

Oh, God, why was he here? To make sure she really, really, *really* understood that he didn't want her?

Well, Lucas, I might have been a little slow on the uptake, but once the message sank in it was there to stay.

"I thought you were the taxi driver. How did you get past the doorman?"

"I didn't. He recognized me." He paused. "From before." Said as if she might not remember their last encounter in this flat. Unfortunately it was burned into her brain with a flamethrower.

She strove for nonchalant. "How's your brother doing?"

"He's out of danger. Looking forward to getting the help he needs. I think being in hospital gave him the shock of a lifetime."

"I'm glad." She was. As hurt and angry as she was at Lucas, she hoped Cora would finally have her father back. "And Cora?"

"She misses you."

Pain sliced through her chest. "Don't. Please."

Lucas glanced to the side where her suitcases sat. "May I come in for a minute?"

"Why?" She didn't think she could take another blow. Not when she was struggling not to memorize every line and crag of that beloved face.

"Because Cora isn't the only one who misses you."

The words took a moment to penetrate her icy heart. Then she started to pick them apart. "You mean Isla and the rest of the staff?"

"Yes, but not just them."

She licked her lips. "Then who?"

Fear buzzed around in her stomach while she waited for him to say something. Anything.

His chest rose as he took a deep breath. "Me. *I* miss you. I don't want you to go."

"You practically offered to pack my bags."

"I was stupid. Scared. My brother is the way he is because he desperately loved his wife. When she died…well, he was never the same. I don't want to end up like that."

She worked through those words. "And you're afraid if you meet someone, you will."

He nodded.

A terrible, wonderful atom of hope split into two. Then three. "Come in."

She stepped aside as he moved into the room and glanced around. Waiting for him to finish and turn back toward her, her brain continued to analyze what it knew. Somehow he'd found out she hadn't left.

Isla.

Darcie had called to tell her that her flight had been delayed. But why would she tell Lucas?

"You say you miss me, that you don't want me to go, but I need something more than that." This time she wasn't willing to settle for less.

He came back and took her hands in his. "I know you do. Which is why I want you to come with me."

"Where?"

"It's a secret. But by the end of it I hope you'll have the answer you need."

The buzzing fear turned into a tornado that whipped through her system and made her doubt. Was he was going to lead her on a merry chase, only to get cold feet again and decide he was better off without her?

Maybe.

So why was that list they'd made a couple of weeks ago stuck in the front pocket of her purse…complete with the smiley face he'd drawn next to the kiss-a-non-triangular-Aussie entry? Because she didn't want to forget. But, like him, she was afraid.

He'd overcome his fear long enough to drive to the flat, though, without knowing what kind of reception he'd get. Didn't she owe it to herself to follow this through to the end? She could always catch that flight tomorrow if it didn't work out.

"Okay, I'll come."

He closed his eyes, the lines between his brows easing. When he opened them again, the brown irises seemed to have warmed to a hue she recognized and loved. A few more atoms split apart, some of them coalescing back together and forming a shape she could almost decipher. He glanced at her clothes. "Can you get those wet?"

"Wet?" Was he going to kill her and toss her lifeless body over the side of his boat? That made her smile. A few more particles merged together. "I think they'll survive."

Twenty minutes later they pulled up to a place she recognized. But it wasn't his boat. "Why are we here?"

"Trust me." He got out of the car and came around to her side and opened the door. She stood on the footpath, staring up at a familiar tower.

"We're going bungee jumping? Now?"

"You're not. I am."

She had no idea what was going on but he'd asked her to trust him. So she walked with him to meet Max, who stood waiting at the entrance. The man pushed his glasses higher on his nose, looking spectacularly pleased with himself for some reason. "Come in. Come in. Everything's ready." He disappeared through the wooden privacy gate.

Lucas murmured, "Remember when you jumped, I waited for you in the pool at the bottom?"

"Yes." She wasn't sure how she got the word out as her throat felt dry and parched.

"I want you to go to the side of the pool and wait for me this time." He gave a half-smile. "Don't ask me why until you've unhooked me."

They went through the gate, a million questions swirling through her mind. Max led her down to the pool, while Lucas climbed the steps to the tower.

She gasped. The water was crystal clear, just as before…but the surface was littered with rose petals. Thousands of them in every color imaginable—red, purple, yellow, white, pink.

Max didn't explain, he just asked her to wait there. "Lucas knows how to unhook himself, but he wants you to go into the water and do it for him this time."

"I don't know how."

The engineer gave her a knowing smile. "He says you do. Just do what your heart tells you."

If she did that, Lucas wouldn't be diving head-first into a pool. They'd be hashing this whole thing out on the couch in her flat. Or in bed, depending on how well the discussion went.

But then Max was gone, joining Lucas in this crazy game of who knew what.

He appeared at the top. His shirt was off. He must have worn swimming trunks underneath his jeans because his tanned legs were on display. He looked strong and powerful. But from the words he'd said back at the flat, he'd hinted he was anything but.

But, then, neither was she. She had her own fears to struggle through. And if they couldn't do it together, then they needed to work on them as separate individuals.

Except those atoms were still dividing. Still joining. She peered, trying to make out what it was becoming. Then, just as Lucas dived far out into the air, arms spread apart, she saw it. It was his face, and the expression on it was similar to the one he had when he looked at Cora. When he looked at his brother.

Love. And fear.

A mixture of two emotions that were intertwined so tightly it was impossible to completely separate them. She knew, because the two were battling it out within her heart as well.

Lucas hurtled toward the pool before being jerked back at the last second, just as he'd been the previous time. The air displaced by his fall made the petals sift over the surface of the water, like ice skaters twirling in colorful costumes. Then the winch began to whine as it slowly lowered Lucas closer to the water. Time for her to get in.

She slipped into the pool, surprised to find some kind of footing where they'd had to tread water before. It felt like wood, but it was high enough that she didn't have to swim, she could simply walk toward him in chest-high water.

When she looked up at him, she found his eyes on her. In their depths was a question. She swallowed, emotion bubbling up in her throat and threatening to escape as a sob. She loved this man. Loved him with all her heart. And she was willing to take him as he was, fears and all, if that's what he wanted.

God, she hoped that was what he wanted.

He didn't say anything, but when he was close enough to touch she gave him a quick kiss on the lips just before his head disappeared beneath the surface, followed by the rest of him. Soon he was hidden from view by the layer of flower petals. Momentary panic went through her. How was she supposed to unhook him? Max hadn't shown her, and Lucas hadn't said anything at all.

Just do what your heart tells you.

Darcie ducked beneath the surface and found him lying on the boards three feet below, the petals shading the area. He could just stand up if he wanted to…it was shallow. But he didn't. She pushed herself down and followed the cord that held his ankles. Unsnapped it. Then the one attached to the harness at his back. It stuck for a second and she wiggled it, suddenly scared he wouldn't come up if she couldn't get it off. There. The hook released.

He was free.

Lucas grabbed hold of her waist and hauled her to the surface, breaking through the layer of velvety petals.

The question he'd told her to ask once he'd completed the jump came out before she could stop it. "Why?"

He pushed damp strands of hair off her face. "Do you remember what it felt like to take that leap?"

She nodded.

"What did you feel?" he murmured, his arm now around her waist.

She thought for a moment, trying to gather her jumbled thoughts. "I was so scared. I didn't want to go through with it, and I felt like screaming the whole way down. But once I reached the pool, and you unhooked me, there was this sense of exhilaration… I can't even describe it."

He nodded. "I know. Because I felt the same things as I sat on the beach with you and started making that list. Terrified. Like I'd lost my stomach, my heart and my head all at once. I fell, and I haven't stopped falling. But I was too afraid to finish it. To let you come alongside me and undo those ropes."

Her eyes watered. She knew exactly what he was talking about. "I feel it too," she whispered. "The fear."

"I love you, Darcie. It took me a while to understand what I'd find once I reached the bottom of that jump—to get past my fear and open my eyes, to really look at what was waiting for me. It was you."

She threw herself into his arms and lifted her lips up for his kiss. It was long and slow and thorough. Once she could breathe again she laid her head on his shoulder. "I love you too, Lucas. You're right, it was scary and making the decision to go over the edge wasn't an easy one. But it was worth it. All of it."

"Yes, it was."

"Hey, Uncle Luke," a voice came from the top of the tower. "When is it my turn to jump?"

Cora stood peering over the edge at them, and even from this distance Darcie could see the little girl's infectious smile.

Laughing, she nipped the bottom of his jaw. "Good thing I didn't leave you there to drown. You were awfully sure of yourself."

"No. I wasn't sure at all. But I hoped."

She hugged him tight. "Aren't you going to answer her question? When can she jump?"

Lucas kissed her cheek, and then shouted back up, "Not for many, many years, sweetheart."

EPILOGUE

WELCOME HOME!

The words, scrawled in pink childish letters and flanked by a heart on either side, greeted them as they opened the door to Lucas's flat.

Three weeks on a beach, and Darcie was still as white as the paper banner. She didn't care. Besides, they hadn't actually spent all that much time sunbathing while in Tahiti. A fact that made her smile.

"Aw, I think I know who wrote that." Darcie twined her arms around her new husband's neck. "But at least we're all alone, because I have something I want to—"

The panicky sound of a throat clearing came from behind the black leather couch, followed by a yip. And then two. A child giggled.

"Oops." Darcie's face heated, as she whispered into his ear. "Not so alone after all."

Lucas made a face at her, just as people came pouring from seemingly every room of the place. The kitchen, the two bedrooms, the veranda. And finally, from behind the couch, appeared Cora, Pete the Geek, Chessa…and Felix.

Cora and Pete launched themselves at the newlyweds and her poor husband *oomphed* as the dog—apparently forgetting everything he'd learned—careened into his side, nearly knocking him down. Darcie barely managed to keep from falling herself.

"Oh, my gosh!" Darcie knelt to hug Cora, peering at the mass of people around them. It looked like most of the MMU staff had turned up for their return—which begged the question: who was minding the maternity unit?

Isla came over and planted a kiss on her cheek as Darcie stood, keeping hold of Cora's hand.

"How was the honeymoon?" her friend asked.

She returned her friend's hug. "Spectacular. How's the baby?"

"Growing like a little weed." She motioned over at Alessandro, who was cradling their infant in his arms. "I barely get to hold him. Flick says Tristan is the same way."

It certainly appeared so, since Tristan had a baby carrier strapped to his chest with his daughter safely ensconced inside it. Flick waved at her.

Darcie gazed around at the people she'd come to know and love over the past year and her eyes threatened to well up, although she somehow forced back the tide. Lucas was still a little spooked by tears. He'd overcome a lot of his fears, but every once in a while he looked at her as if afraid she might disappear into the ether.

And she might. But that's not how she planned to live her life. And she certainly wasn't going to let her husband dwell on it either.

Then her eyes widened as her gaze skimmed the rest of the room.

There, still standing behind the couch, were

Felix and Chessa. And the childminder had a certain pink tinge to her cheeks that looked familiar. And— Oh… *Oh!* Felix's arm was slung casually around the woman's waist. It looked like she and Lucas hadn't been the only ones who'd been busy over the past couple of months.

Felix had completed his rehab program a few weeks before the wedding and had been on the straight and narrow ever since, according to the texts they'd got from Chessa. But she hadn't mentioned anything about a budding romance.

As if noticing her attention was elsewhere, Lucas glanced up from the group of people he was chatting with and caught her eye. She nodded in Felix's direction. She saw the moment he digested what he was seeing. His Adam's apple dipped. And then he was moving, catching his brother up in a fierce hug that was full of happiness.

And hope.

It was the best gift anyone could have given him—seeing his brother on the cusp of a bright new future. And little did Lucas know that another surprise awaited him. One she'd postponed telling him until just the right moment.

That moment was now. He could handle it. They both could.

When the tears came this time she didn't stop them, feeling Isla's arm come around her waist and squeeze. "It's wonderful, isn't it?"

"Yes."

Before she could say anything else he was back, grabbing her to him, his breathing rough and unsteady.

"Lucas." Her fingers buried themselves in the hair at the back of his head, praying she was doing the right thing as she leaned up to whisper, "I know it's early, but our friends aren't the only ones having babies."

He leaned back and looked at her for a long second, a question in his eyes. She gave a single nod.

"I love you," was all he said, before he drew her back against him, burying his face in her neck.

And when she felt moisture against her skin,

she knew it was going to be okay. Her big-hearted husband was finally ready to accept that the world could be a good place. It brought sadness at times, yes, but it was also full of kindness and laughter and contentment.

All because they'd dared to do something outrageous and wild and completely dangerous: they'd fallen in love.

* * * * *

This is the final story in the fabulous
MIDWIVES ON-CALL *series.*
Make sure you've picked up all 8 books!